THE LEGEND
OF THE
WHITE LEOPARD
AND
OTHER STORIES

BEN O'LEE

PAGE PUBLISHING, INC.
Conneaut Lake, PA

First originally published by Page Publishing 2020

ISBN 978-1-64701-647-0 (pbk)
ISBN 978-1-64701-648-7 (digital)

Printed in the United States of America

DEDICATION

To the Creator of the Universe;
my lovely parents Canice and Philomena; my siblings and friends.
Lastly, you, the reader.

CONTENTS

THE LEGEND OF THE WHITE LEOPARD

Our children may learn about the heroes of the past. Our task is to make ourselves the architects of the future.

—Jomo Kenyatta

CHARACTER LIST

Jaali—medicine man (*mugad*); seer (*kiruria*)
Sia—wife of Jaali
Gitonga—father of Jomo
Mumbi—wife of Gitonga
Jomo—son of Gitonga
Zawadi—wife of Jomo
Wangai—daughter of Jomo
Mimi—daughter of Jomo
Patrick—son of Jomo
Craig—pharmacologist
Campbell—scientist
Simaya—mother of cubs
Ajabu—male cub
Lebo—female cub one
Kivu—female cub two

Once upon a nightly sky gaze in the cold winter nights on Mount Kenya, Simaya the Leopard groaned in pains. Whispering sounds through the cracks and caves were the only reprieve during that final push for the last cub. Ajabu was the only male and the last of three cubs. Illuminated by the sickle moon, the lonely cave harmonized melodies of the crying cubs. At long last, Simaya's legacy was not to be forgotten!

Across the northeastern slopes of the mountain, Jaali, the great medicine man (*mugad*) and seer (*kiruria*), lived among the Meru people. Attaining such a status was no mean feat. Jaali's pedigree as a *kiruria* dated back three centuries of spoken and proven manifestations of life-changing events. The events that led to the abolishment of unpleasant female customary practices in Meru and the establishment of an all-female settlement in faraway Umoja in 1990 were fresh reminders. Profound premonitions uttered, however, came with a price.

Sia's nights had been short and worrisome for the bed they shared was transformed to a stage for Jaali's macabre-like dance. Ducking from flailing arms in between short snoozes had become the order of the day—at least before Jaali's second annual trek to the mountain. Before sunrise, Sia fixed Jaali his usual cup of tea and set it on a stool close to their bed.

"*Asante!*" Jaali said.

"*Uliamkaje!* Did you sleep well?" Sia asked.

"Yes, I did. But I have been restless, and I hear the voices of our ancestors," a confused Jaali said.

"Eh! Jaali, those ancestors of yours better dance alone. Have you thought of your daughters and our little grandchildren?" Sia responded with her arms akimbo.

"Sia, it seems your hysteria increases with age. I can't imagine what would become of me when you get past sixty years." Jaali teased.

"Not dancing in my sleep, that's for sure," Sia replied.

Jaali shook his head and began sipping his tea. "I have to travel in two days," he said.

"But how—" Sia said before she was cut off.

"I am meeting with the *mzungus* for business. They need our herbs," Jaali said.

"*Haiya*! It's so sudden," Sia reacted.

"I must be on my way to Gitonga's, this can't wait for another day."

*****

Fortunately, Simaya gained enough pounds before evading the poachers' Dane guns, and her recovery was vital to ensure milk flow for the fledgling cubs. The temperature this night was at a freezing point; patchy snowflakes lit the rocky mountain like fluorescent trackers. Simaya trekked miles before striking an antelope. With the antelope fastened in her jaws, she made for home—in time for her cubs' supper.

By mid-January, three months after birthing, Simaya's cubs grew restless. Not even Simaya's growl could deter them from their determination as they poked and clawed their mother's mammary for the last drop of milk. The third week was quite a remarkable and curious night for Simaya. Guided by her keen sense of smell, she led her cubs down the gentle eastward slopes of the mountain. When they reached the foot of the mountain, she sniffed the cubs, and they were complete. Just ahead of the grassland was Gitonga's homestead.

As they approached the oak tree, barren clouds gave way to a vibrant moon. Simaya paused to smell the air around—saturated with the lingering aroma of Sia's corn pudding, beef stew, and wild rice. In another breath, it smelled the mustiness of the farm animals. Her exuberant cubs did not make for good company as they alerted the nearby mongrels, but her subtle growl silenced them. Simaya rested on her hinds as if to contemplate the next plan of actions when suddenly, Ajabu ran after a bush rat. The full glare of the moon exposed Simaya's gold-flamed eyes, which were fixed and wide; she noticed something strange. Ajabu's coat was different from the rest of her cubs. Its measured gait toward Ajabu signaled a change in demeanor. Lebo and Kivu (the other cubs) followed after her. Simaya's fortunate experience as a second-time mother was enough to spot any anomaly but could be excused for not noticing Ajabu's difference at birth because of the cubs' lanugo hair.

Simaya ran her moist nostrils all the way to Ajabu's tail head-first and did the same for the others: their pheromones were alike. Ajabu's white fur was a consequence of a rare feline genetic anomaly—albinism. Simaya's snout retracted to expose its fangs and gave Ajabu a jab that left it scampering. The other cubs huddled among themselves, frightened. Next, Simaya steered Lebo and Kivu in the opposite direction. Anytime Ajabu trailed them, Simaya responded with a growl. Dejected and vulnerable, Ajabu was banished from the pride. Crestfallen, Ajabu roamed the compound of Gitonga, hoping to make do with some leftovers.

*****

The unfinished road traversing the fringes of Gitonga's cottage was an ancestral route, conveying all manner of people. Sunrays that bounced off a mirror in the room illuminated his prominent forehead, denying him any time to gaze at the ceiling. The front view of his cottage faced the "sacred mountain." Gitonga was awakened by the early morning commute and the chatter of tribal, market women along with young lads and ladies, all vying for a shot at a better life. Gitonga was not one to sleep deeply because his tactile senses were superb: even a crawling bug on the bed could rouse him. With his lanky frame that spanned across the bed, it was easy for him to feel the slightest movement. But Mumbi, his wife, had other crafty ways of sneaking out of bed. Gakoromone Farmers' Market favored early birds if she was to buy fresh produce.

Gitonga opened the glass shutters and was surprised to see heading his way, a six-foot-tall, dark, and trimmed man: it was the great *mugad*! Whosoever you asked, Jaali walked with a serpentine staff with one hand behind his back, acknowledging every salutation with a nod. Worthless words were anathema to Jaali whose travels were restricted to the twilight of dawn and sunrise. Whenever the great *mugad* made inroads by daylight, he would trot like a jackal as though under the influence of an extraterrestrial power.

"Great *mugad*! I greet you! May you come inside?" Gitonga insisted.

"Thank you, my son, the reason for my visit is not one for merrymaking," Jaali responded.

"I am all ears, great *mugad*."

Jaali cleared his throat. "The spirits of our enemies have taken a strange form and it has come to take a soul from our community."

Gitonga listened intently, but deep inside, he was alarmed. *Eh! My enemies are at it again!*

"These spirits hover around, seeking to provoke. Pretend like you don't see or hear them so that you don't give them a face in your household!" Jaali concluded.

Gitonga sighed. "Your message is well received, *mugad*."

Before Jaali departed, he stalled for a moment and asked, "Where is your son?"

"He has not been here in over a month," Gitonga responded.

Jaali shook his head and departed to prepare ahead for the journey.

*****

Gitonga forgot he had a cup of water in his hands. With a mouthful of water, he gargled then walked across from the room to the backyard. Ajabu's footprints appeared on one side at the back of the house. *My cows! The goats! Haiya, the chickens!* Gitonga ran toward the animal pen. There were neither bloodstains, chicken feathers, nor a sign of destruction to suggest predation; the footprints ended underneath the pawpaw tree. *Perhaps the sounds of the animals scared Ajabu as it strayed toward the animal pen,* Gitonga thought. He was relieved and returned from the house with a machete, hoping to strike down a band of alley cats if the need arose.

Mumbi hurriedly paid the taxi driver as soon as she saw her husband striding heavily around the compound. *Sielewi* (I don't understand)! *Who must have upset him?* she thought while dropping her shopping bags by the entrance door.

"Please, give me that thing before you hurt someone," Mumbi demanded. "What happened?"

"Come see for yourself," Gitonga insisted.

"Eh! What do these cats want?" she asked. "But it's no reason for this machete."

"Mumbi, have you seen a cat's footprint? Do they look like those of cats?" Gitonga asked.

Without further ado, Gitonga narrated Jaali's odd visit to his wife Mumbi, and as they discussed, Jomo drove into the compound. Mumbi was advised not to speak about it to their son.

"Baba, Mama, *Uliamkaje!*" Jomo hailed.

"*Mzuri!*" both replied.

"Is anything the matter?" he asked as he observed their countenances.

"No, son, I was only telling your father that prices in the market have become steep," she replied.

"Yeah, tell me about it," Jomo retorted.

"How much longer will I ask to see my grandchildren?" Gitonga interjected.

"*Haiya!* Not again. Can he settle in before the question?" Mumbi asked.

"Do I have to remind him that my grandchildren need to appreciate their culture?"

"It's been a hectic morning. I had better prepare lunch while you two can entertain yourselves."

"It is okay, Mama, Baba's always right. Anything to eat, Mama?"

"Help yourself with some fruits before the food is ready."

"That wouldn't be a bad idea, but I feel for some pawpaw."

Jomo picked up a thin, lengthy, medium-sized branch with a hook at its tip, which rested on the wall to his left. He anchored the hooklike tip around the stalk of the pawpaw fruit. Two firm tugs sent one fruit after another tumbling down. Confusion was written all over his face as he stooped to pick the fruits. *Good gracious! Heaven help us!*

"Ah! Those papaws look nice and ripe, let me cut them up for you," Mumbi requested.

Jomo handed the fruits to her and watched to see if there was more to glean from his mother's demeanor.

"Mama, you shouldn't allow your new pets to roam around, they could be endangered."

Mumbi glanced at him, not sure what he meant, and continued cutting the fruit. He picked up the bowl of fruit and set it on the coffee table to share with his father.

"So, Baba, have you thought over my proposition?" Jomo asked.

"What proposition?" Gitonga asked. "I could hardly keep up with the things you say," he continued.

Jomo let out a sigh and said, "Upgrading the animal pens and installing novel equipment to improve yield."

"Have you come to change the way I do things to pay for your wife's wasteful lifestyle?" Gitonga grumbled.

"Zawadi is my wife and my choice, please, leave her out of this!" Jomo replied.

"Why should I? She is the reason why I haven't seen my grand-children in six months!"

"Maybe if you were more hospitable to her, the kids would've kept you company!"

"Enough!" Mumbi interjected. "Lunch is served."

"Patricia was your choice and not mine. Zawadi is my decision and mine alone!" Jomo affirmed. "Mama, I'd better be on my way…"

"Don't tell me I cooked this meal for nothing?"

"He has become lily-livered. Let him go! Kikuyu blood runs through his veins, he must recognize that." Gitonga dismissed with a wave of the hand.

*****

By the third day, Jaali emerged from the secluded chamber behind his house: a place where he fed once a day aside from the daily carbohydrate-packed meals, five days prior to his departure. Seclusion ensured readiness both mentally and physically; in addi-tion, he gained clarity and revelation on the kinds of herb combi-nations. Jaali's successes on these daunting trips were a credit to his wife, Sia, who was a honeybee farmer and gifted craftswoman weaving mats, sling bags, and hats from sisal fibers, which Jaali used on his trips. The morning before any trip, she would smoke four pounds of steak (one chunk a pound per day) on charcoal wood and by night, wrap them with special leaves for preservation. To complete the meal package, she would include *ugali* (corn meal), sun-dried dates, and a leather bottle with fresh goat milk.

Jaali slung his sisal bag, wore his hat, and fastened his leather bottle and waist pouch around his belt (on opposite sides). When all was set, he stepped outside and saw glimpses of golden rays eager to break forth from the horizon: the timing was perfect!

"Travel safe, and may our Creator guide you back safely," Sia said.

Jaali waved in acknowledgment, rolled out his bicycle, and rode into the twilight of the morning. The four-day journey to the top of Mount Kenya had begun.

Jaali's divination revealed the routes from Chogoria to Point Lenana. Before noon, he arrived at Chogoria town and proceeded along a trail lined by bamboo trees on both sides. Along the outer edge of the entrance, he concealed the bicycle from prying eyes. Felled bamboo sticks in the forest a few feet away grew antimalarial plants; he pulled his knife, cut the plant, and slid it into the sisal bag wrapped in banana leaves. The sun was majestic but prickly while sweat drops failed to soothe his dark skin. Jaali veered off the footpath to rest for a drink and have his first steak and *ugali* meal and ate a few dates (after a trek that lasted three hours, ten kilometers by foot, and an ascent at 950 meters high). He reached Lake Elice by sundown and unfolded a mat and cloth then tucked the bags underneath his body and rested for the night.

*****

Ajabu returned the following night to scavenge for food. It made do with millet pulps laid out to air-dry and remnants from chicken parts that Mumbi discarded. After having its fill, it sniffed around and drank water from an aluminum bowl, accidentally knocking it over. The clanking noise woke Mumbi who was the last to retreat to bed.

"Gitonga, wake up!" Mumbi beckoned.

"Eh! What's the matter? Can I get some sleep?" he asked.

"Shhhh! someone is in the backyard," she said.

Gitonga rose from the bed speedily, put on a shirt, and rushed to the back of the house. For only a fraction of seconds, Ajabu's flaming eyes met Gitonga's. He pelted Ajabu with a rock the size of a grapefruit. The impact left Ajabu squealing as it darted to safety with a limp, which sent the mongrels in the neighborhood into a howling frenzy.

Mumbi asked while peeping from the door, "What was that?"

"That's one strange-looking animal. I have never seen a thing like that!" Gitonga replied.

Gitonga and Mumbi spent the night with apprehension, startling at any sudden noise outside the house.

Wounded and in pains, Ajabu made its way to the forest bordering the Meru axis of the mountain where safety and recovery are assured. Survival, however, was a game of chance in the wild.

*****

On day 2 before sunrise, Jaali was back on the trail after washing his face by a puddle of water close by. Within a few meters, he stopped to assess the landscape of low-lying, sunbaked straw grasses. Jaali walked across to the side when he set his sight on an aged African green heart pepper tree (*Warburgia ugandensis*) and peeled a substantial amount off its bark then wrapped and stowed it away in his bag. Four hours later, he reached Nithi gates by sundown, unpacked his bag, and ate the second meal pack and stargazed before falling asleep on his mat. (He was aware of the open field, so he brought along three sticks and made a tripod for his makeshift tent.) The day before the journey, his divination revealed a particular location to extract *Warburgia ugandensis* an important plant.

On day 3, the windy morning had a slight chill to it, so Jaali's trek was delayed for sunrise. It was sufficient time enough to have the third meal. Reenergized and refreshed, he packed up his make-shift tent and headed for the waterfalls; there, he stopped to refill his bottle with water. On a tree, along the slope of the waterfall, a tan-colored, checkered owl perched. Instantly, he recognized the tree from the vision. Gently he descended the slopes of the rock to cut a few leaves. The sun was blazing hot, and he decided to rest inside a cave close by the rocks. Four wandering Skye monkeys observed with intent as he cooled off with a few gulps of water. Jaali let down his mat and placed his walking stick and medicine bag to his side and fell asleep. Gradually the monkeys approached, and in a moment, the male monkey launched an audacious bid and snatched his medicine bag filled with the finest medicinal herbs.

Thirty minutes later, Jaali woke up from his nap, yawning and stretching. *My eyes can't see this calamity! My bag is gone!* Everything happened so fast for him to comprehend. Inside his leather waist pouch, he removed a white chalk, drew some lines on the floor, and painted around his right eye with the chalk. Jaali recited invocations for a few minutes and became silent: his eyes opened! He packed what was left of his gear and ran in the direction of the monkeys. When he came up to Lake Michaelson in pursuit of the monkeys, his breath began to shorten as the monkeys were about to throw it into the lake. A crowned eagle swooped down and snatched the bag, but Jaali could not afford to lose the contents in the bag. So he threw the first rock and missed, but his second attempt stunned the eagle. The display that transpired next was simply one of nature's finest! Another eagle of its kind plunged from dizzy heights and clawed it back upward. The first eagle regained composure, then the second one released its grip and they flew in the direction of Point Lenana. All his life, Jaali had never seen such a spectacle. Even if he ignored the contents of the bag, the awareness that his sustenance rest in the clutches of a bird was beyond incomprehensible! In no time, he was on the eagle's trail.

*****

Back in Nova Scotia, Goldsmith & Levine Pharmaceuticals (G&L) recorded significant success in the preclinical trial of *Warburgia ugandensis* for the treatment of resistant malaria. The success of this trial owes credence to a young Scottish pharmacologist, Craig Morrison. G&L paired Craig with a cancer researcher from the University of Glasgow.

"You must be Mr. Craig?"

"Yes, I am," Craig replied. "Good afternoon! Mr. Campbell, I suppose?"

Campbell grinned and shook hands with Craig. "Come along, we got only two days on our hands before the trip," Craig said, leading the way to his office.

"Care for tea?" Craig asked.

"I am stuffed, but thanks for the offer," Campbell replied.

"So, Craig, tell me about this trip." He reclined on the chair. "Does that include a safari trip?"

Craig stopped steeping his tea to chuckle. "You certainly think this is a fun trip? Well, there is a possibility we might if our meeting ends on time?"

"What meeting?" Campbell asked.

Craig sipped his sea and sat down. "With the *mugad*," he said.

Campbell thought for a second, he heard "mu guards." "Who the heck are these guards?"

Craig tried to be as cordial as he could tolerate. "He is a diviner and traditional medicine man with an outstanding knowledge of curative herbs."

Craig was a good judge of character, and he was right about this fellow.

Since 1985, Craig developed a good rapport with Jaali while studying abroad for a semester at the University of Nairobi. As a student, he developed a keen interest in the ecosystem in and around Mount Kenya. On one of his expeditions, he heard of a *mugad* with an extraordinary understanding of herbal plants. Jaali's initial unwillingness to give audience to the Scotsman was doused by his humility and enthusiasm.

Craig's role was vital for the pharmaceutical company and the Meru community. The freedom he was given on the project enabled him to create a working relationship based on mutual trust, which secured a memorandum of understanding (MOU) to establish the Greenbark Pharmaceuticals. Topmost in the minds of G&L executives was the establishment of a drug manufacturing plant focused on processing and preserving the natural qualities of herbs (after purification) by crushing them into powder forms and press them into capsules, as well as boost the cultivation and forest conservation of these herbs. Then, the indigenous people would determine the prices of medicine sold to other countries, and in exchange, G&L would enjoy tax waivers and 30 percent profit for products marketed outside the country.

*****

On day 4, stretched to exhaustion, Jaali stumbled over a tree stump and landed on a sharp stick that left a gash. The pain was lancinating, and as he rolled over to the left, warm fluid streamed across his right calf (above his boots). Jaali reached for his snuffbox in his leather pouch and scooped a generous amount of crushed herbs and placed around the cut. Within five minutes, the blood stopped oozing, and he secured it with a strip of cloth. After quenching his thirst, the cool breeze that swept through put him to sleep.

Sounds of chirping crickets, coupled with the aromatic scent of the passion fruits around, awakened him in the middle of the night. Having such a rest gives room for acclimatization. Before leaving for Point Lenana via Mintos Hut, Jaali had his fill of passion fruits. As he approached his via point, he felt short-winded and fell by the side of the tarn.

On day 5, in the early hours of the morning (about 6:00 a.m.), Jaali dreamed of Sia's savory cooking. Just before he got up, the wind blew hither, bringing along some aroma. And when he stood, his eyes locked in on a parcel-like substance. It was the last meal in the bag before the mishap. In less than five minutes, his digestive juices waited in anticipation. Next, he scoured the grassland, unsure of what to expect. Over ten feet radius, the bag laid on top a hedge, and he hurried toward it. Fortunately, the wrapped meal—being heavier than the other contents—fell from the bag when the crown eagle was in flight. The eagle must have been hurt and was unable to carry the bag any further as blood splattered on the bag. Time was of importance for the *muzungus* were to arrive the next day. Fortunately, the herbs were still intact; he tied the loose strings of the bag.

Soon enough he shut his eyes for five minutes to search for inner guidance. Jaali felt a nudge then raced ahead to an unfamiliar landmark, the Square Turn. From this location, instincts took full control: a familiar gust of wind swept by as he descended from the eastern slopes.

At home, a worried Sia paced the compound, looking out for Jaali at every sighting of human perambulation. Beneath the half-hearted compliments returned to passersby, Sia's thoughts harbored all manner of dreadful possibilities: *Jaali's muscle mass was enough for animals to desire him. Who will put up with these chatty lips of mine?*

Down the path, Jaali was shielded from the scorching sun by an overcast sky. Approximately three hours on the trail, Theemwe was in view.

Jaali reached the ancestral path that traversed Gitonga's abode, feeling exhausted. Gitonga watched the last goat enter the pen when he saw Jaali stoop to catch his breath. Even though Jaali was tired, the ancestral spirits beckoned him to turn his head in the direction of Gitonga's abode. Suddenly, the air was still, and a roar echoed from a distance. The hairs on Gitonga's skin stood erect and caused friction with his clothing, crackling with every motion. He was glued to the thatched gate of the goat pen for he was not ready to incur any wrath (if any existed).

Mumbi wondered what took her husband so long to return to the house, so she hollered, "Gitonga! What's taking you so long?"

This wife of mine, please, don't come this way, a panicked Gitonga thought. She headed for the pen just as Gitonga feared. His furious hand wave to deter his wife from approaching the location was futile. Jaali heard her voice and walked away with a disapproving nod.

"Mumbi, if doom befalls us, then you know you caused it," Gitonga said.

"My love, what have I done?" Mumbi replied.

"Did you see Jaali?" Gitonga asked.

"Was I supposed to see him?" Mumbi responded.

"How would you have seen him when you were busy yelling my name like a town crier," Gitonga said. "Thanks to you, he was upset when he heard your voice."

Mumbi was confused but shrugged it aside and went about preparing dinner.

*****

Sia spotted her husband before he arrived at the house and raced toward him; the impact of the embrace nearly knocked him down. On the spot, she took possession of all he carried with the exception of his serpentine-looking staff. She knew Jaali too well to let him walk without assistance to the house. After a cold bath and a hot meal, Jaali was brief recounting his ordeal and retired for the night because the *muzungus* from G&L would stop by the next morning.

At five o'clock the following morning, Jaali retreated to his inner chamber for another session of divination. Two hours later, Sia knocked at the door. "Your visitors are here," she said.

She opened the door and departed, leaving behind the *muzungus*. The chest-level entrance door to Jaali's chamber was no accidental construction; it humbled the proud upon entry. Craig understood the protocol, but Campbell, the ginger-haired scientist, refused to enter. It was not surprising because he possessed an ego the size of his body. A livid Craig made his way outside.

"Hey, look here, stranger, nobody cares if you were trained in Cambridge or Oxford. You must accord our host the respect he deserves," Craig said.

"So you mean I should force myself through this substandard doorpost?" Campbell responded.

"You have two choices, you either go inside or bust it. If you chose the latter, then, I'd see you in Nova Scotia," Craig murmured.

Campbell reluctantly followed Craig behind.

"Great *mugad*!" Craig hailed. "We salute you!"

"Yeah right!" Campbell laughed.

The menacing expression on Craig's face spoke more words than action. Jaali returned the compliments with a clenched fist across his heart.

"Your friend is a greenhorn, isn't he?" Jaali asked.

"Oh, he speaks good English?" Campbell said.

The eyes on Craig's crimson-colored face widened, and he was a few moments from smacking down the back of Campbell's head when Jaali intervened, motioning his hand.

"Better English than you imagined. Only a fool thinks he has answers to all the questions of human problems," Jaali said.

The whistling wind was felt as it swept through the cross-ventilated chamber, bringing with it the cooing sounds of the doves nearby.

"I grew up in an era where boys longed to be men, when great men were judged in the open by their might. Did your bulging eyes see eggs explode like firecrackers? Have you ever, in your protected and sheltered youth, seen warriors, men of valor battle bare fist for supremacy? Could a man like you hold your nerves when men walked on spiked nails bare feet? If you have not, be quiet!" Jaali thundered.

"Voodoo is all I see," Campbell snickered.

Swiftly, Jaali stumped his serpentine stick on the floor. The stare from the *mugad* sent shock waves down Campbell's feeble spine and cracked open his urethral sphincters.

"Great *mugad*," Craig hailed, "please, excuse the impetuous ignorance of my colleague. I am here for what we discussed earlier."

Jaali reached for his medicine bag and drew it close to his seat. Campbell's heart must have clocked close to a mile with every move Jaali made.

One plant at a time, Jaali described the herbs and their medicinal properties. *Warburgia ugandensis* was of prime importance to Craig for he was in the last phase of the clinical trial. Jaali paused for a moment, then he paired *Warburgia ugandensis* with a portion of the antimalarial and anti-HSV herbs (*Carissa edulis*).

"These herbs must be soaked in brine and boiled at 50°F. Leave the solution to soak for a day and pour the extract and leave to cool at room temperature. It should be taken first thing before a meal and the last thing before bedtime for two months."

Jaali and Craig had established a relationship founded over seven solid years. When Craig was done with his entry, Jaali motioned to him to come close. He whispered a few words into Craig's ears, which left him perplexed. *Oh, Lord of heavens, deliver me from the lion's den. I beg thee...*were the supplications of a terrified bigot, Campbell.

It took Craig a few minutes to process the information. He reached out his hand for a handshake; Jaali, in acknowledgment, returned the gesture with a firm squeeze. With Campbell's etiquette being fast-tracked, the two Scotsmen took a bow and departed.

Five minutes of head bobbing inside a 1993 Jeep Wrangler was a spooky ride. All sorts of thoughts overwhelmed Campbell, especially the image of Jaali's whispering, and he couldn't hide his trepidations.

"You might want to start saying something, my nerves can't take anymore," Campbell said.

Nothing but blaring horns and the waving hands of the locals whom Craig was accustomed made for good company.

"Are we gonna be ambushed by the locals? Say something, god-damnit!" Campbell demanded, grabbing his shirt.

"No! Far from it," a reluctant Craig said.

"Then what is it?"

Craig gave him a scathing stare and said, "It's personal."

They returned to the hotel room like sour bedmates to catch a quick nap before the safari tour.

*****

Gitonga sat in the living room with his wife absorbed in the memories of their love. They were very fond of each other then and now despite their growing family. The thought of Jaali sighting them kissing under a mango tree still sends shivers down their spine. She recalled Gitonga's bicycle rides in search of her in the boardinghouse for females and the rented tuxedo he wore to impress her on occasions, including moments their children came along.

Jomo arrived to check up on them and to find out if his mother had spoken to his father regarding the idea of setting up an animal husbandry. He also observed to see if he would get any other incline regarding the footprints from the other day, but was kept in the dark of happenings.

Seven months later, Ajabus's miraculous healing and survival in the forest was a remarkable tale of resilience. Ajabu returned to Gitonga's residence, walking stealthily and stooping beneath the shrubs. Before long, it climbed up the nearest oak tree and observed Gitonga herding his goats and cattle in to the pen at sundown. Ajabu continued to observe Gitonga's routine for another day or two.

Meanwhile, Jaali paced about the sitting room where Sia sat; he moved like a jackal from end to end. Sia was anxious for him.

"Do you hear anything?" Jaali asked.

Sia was confused and feared her husband had become schizophrenic.

"I don't hear anything," she responded. "Please, don't tell me your ancestors are calling or else I'll give you some of your herbs to drink."

*****

At about 10:00 p.m., Ajabu descended from the oak tree to the ground and strutted with a menacing gait, with gold-flamed eyes peering through the landscape. Hidden behind those flaming eyes were memories of abandonment and pain yearning to be extinguished, but with a price.

Ajabu's gentle pace increased with every meter it strode. As it arrived at Gitonga's house, it went straight to the goat pen and tore down the thatched gate and pounced on a goat as it cried for mercy. Its attack was swift and decisive. Undeterred by the relentless howls by mongrels, it reached for the neck of another male goat and suffocated by crushing its windpipe as its jaws closed in. Ajabu dragged its kill along its trail and up the tree from where it descended. The climb to the treetop took three flights, resting the dead goat along the junction of a wide branch. Blood-sniffing dogs waited patiently beneath the tree for the leftovers to drop.

Gitonga heard the bleats behind the house, but the sumptuous *ugali* meal, steak, and the local moonshine, *chang'aa*, which he indulged, left him half-seas over. Mumbi bouts of craze when he got drunk were all too familiar to Gitonga. Often, she wondered if his optic nerves and brain were charred by the lethal mix of fermented maize and sorghum when he sent flower vases and miniature-sized crafts tumbling to the ground in search of his bearing. So on this night, he was not perturbed about his wife's hysteria for it was typical of her.

Mumbi was halfway through the morning chores but was alarmed at the sight of the carnage. To think that she would rush back and shake up Gitonga to his senses was the logical thing to do, it was by no means a long shot; instead, she opted to wrap her hands around her head and scream at the top of her voice. Soon enough, Gitonga flipped over from his bed and rushed toward the bellow. By eyeballing the goat pen, he noticed that one more billy goat out of his ten was missing from the mix. Mumbi rushed into the house and placed a call to Jomo; he arrived in less than an hour.

"Baba, if you only listened to me, this wouldn't have happened."

Gitonga turned to give Mumbi the stare to last a lifetime, but she turned her face in the opposite direction; then he responded, "No!"

One couldn't have imagined what unfolded the following day. About the same time, Ajabu made its first kill, and it galloped toward the homestead of a sworn enemy. Gitonga was on a tipsy streak, haggling over trivialities when the unforgiving feline closed in on his pheromones. In a fit of rage, Ajabu sprang up on its hind legs, and from behind, a loud *smash! crack!* and *tinkle* dispersed pieces of louvers in all directions.

Mumbi let out a huge cry. "Gitonga, he is climbing…"

Gitonga staggered to the floor from the sofa, and his startled eyes met Ajabu's flickering yellow-gold iris as it roared ferociously. Mumbi reached for a cast iron skillet and smacked Ajabu on the face as it attempted to claw its way in through the window frames. Mumbi hauled Gitonga away frantically from harm's way. She removed her blouse and applied pressure at the nape of his neck to stop the bleeding. Wriggling and stunned, Ajabu reattempted its climb, but misjudged its leap onto the base of the window panel.

One thing on Mumbi's mind was to get help. She moved him to the side and rushed to the phone to call Jomo. "The *Chui* just attacked—" and Gitonga yanked the phone wire off the wall. His actions were to Mumbi an impossible thought. She was lost for words. Jomo's sudden reaction as he rushed out bed startled his wife, Zawadi.

"Can you tell me what's going on?" Zawadi asked.

He rushed for the car keys soon after he wore a shirt over his barren torso.

"There's a situation at home, something about a leopard," he replied, running out of the house.

Mumbi's fit of hysteria was of epic proportions—hurling all manner of tirades at the irrational Gitonga. Before they could react, Ajabu leaped with a ferocious roar once more at the window panel. Unfortunately, the pieces of broken glasses hampered its claws from latching on the wall. Gitonga's instinct kicked in. He grabbed the rotary phone and flung toward Ajabu's face with accuracy, knocking Ajabu backward to the ground, then it scurried away. Mother luck was on their side, but if you asked Gitonga, he would rather lecture one that they were saved because Leopards fear Kikuyu warriors than remodeling his animal pens.

Jomo arrived at his parents' house within thirty minutes and headed for the living room. One could not mistake the expression of relief on Mumbi's face on sighting Jomo. In turn, his mother's tight squeeze came close to the feeling of welcoming the proverbial prodigal son.

"Baba! Mama!" Jomo yelled. "Where is it?" he asked.

The blood-splattered walls shed light on the extent of the injury.

"Are you both all right?" Jomo asked.

"I have a cut under my foot, but your dad needs more help with the cut behind his neck," his mom replied.

Mumbi could hear Gitonga mumbling and grumbling underneath his breath.

"I wonder what it would take for you to give in to your foolish pride," Mumbi taunted. "This pride of yours put us at the mercy of the jaws of death."

A furious Gitonga departed saying, "A thoroughbred Kikuyu needs no help from a suckling babe!"

Mumbi still couldn't wrap her head around her headstrong husband's reluctance. "If a second attack happens, you would know when a woman had enough!" Mumbi threatened.

"Not a problem, Mama, some people chose not to be helped even when death is inevitable!"

"Shut that trap of yours, young man!" Gitonga raged.

"Unlike you, Baba, I'm willing to put aside my differences to dialogue."

A petulant Gitonga allowed his son to clean the wound and remove the piece of glass lodged at the nape of his neck. After cleansing the cut and treating with an antibacterial ointment, he applied pressure with gauze then secured it with a wide Band-Aid.

At night, while Jomo was in one of the rooms in his father's house, Mumbi softened her approach on the matter concerning Jomo's request. Gitonga, in general, was a man difficult to please, but Mumbi knew how best to make inroads to his fenced heart. Like a pro golfer, she unleashed master strokes of eulogies that reached dizzying heights before he finally cracked a smile. For the rest of the night, he pondered over the matter.

Jomo passed the night at his parents' and was awakened in the morning upon Gitonga's beckoning. At last, his father came around! It was a step, at least by Jomo's imagination, in the right direction.

In the coming days, Jomo drew up a plan and the cost of transforming the farmland into a modern one. A second attack two days later by Ajabu on another goat petrified the family and hastened the planned reformation. More than ever, all hands must be on deck for this project to succeed.

*****

Goldsmith & Levine, Nova Scotia

Craig's role was about to change following the successful completion of the first clinical trial of *Warburgia ugandensis*. G&L finalized a plan to develop and mass produce *Warburgia ugandensis* as an alternative or adjunct treatment for the treatment of HIV-related diseases. Craig was excited yet reluctant to accept the new role. His reluctance to accept the new role did not come as a surprise: he insisted that representatives of the Meru community be present to review the contents of the MOU before signing. Jomo's insistence paid off. Officials from the Department of Wildlife Conservation, Ministry of Health, Department of Agriculture, and Jomo were present at the signing.

The deal between G&L Pharmaceuticals was negotiated without breaking a sweat, all thanks to Jaali's longtime trusted friend. Craig had visited Meru without any colleagues in order to confide in Jaali about the future of alternative medicine in Meru and, most importantly, the *mugad's* legacy. Jaali's trust in Craig epitomized respect for individual differences, religious, and cultural perspectives—in many ways tried and true. Both were convinced that the future of Meru spelled prosperity.

Simultaneously, plans by the Kenyan government to establish the Greenbark Pharmaceuticals in Meru were concluded. For this project to commence, a worthy Meru son must oversee this project. The search was brief: Jomo was appointed the project manager. This project was the first of its kind and, if successful, would be a model for the region, continent, and perhaps the world.

*****

At Gitonga's residence, the persistence of Ajabu and its relentless attacks on goats and now cattle left no one in doubt that human casualties were increasingly inevitable. Jomo, in conjunction with the Department of Wildlife Conservation, swung into action: Ajabu's next attack was imminent. A wide net was hoisted on high-hanging branches below the entrance of the pen; its ends were fastened on four branches (two on each side), stretched nearly to breaking points. Not leaving anything to chance, a trapdoor cage was set along the path of recent footprints. Beneath the black-veiled cage, pieces of freshly cut goat parts were spread inside the cage, which was situated at the entrance of the goat pen.

The atmosphere this particular night was still and thick. One fact was certain: the leopard's uncanny pattern of attack blighted the confidence of the trap-setting park rangers who lay in wait at Gitonga's residence.

About 10:00 p.m., Ajabu descended from its accustomed tree and began walking. Its brisk pace across the patchy grassland slowed halfway through to Gitonga's residence. For every foot it gained, there was a slight pause to sniff the air around. Unusually, the lights at Gitonga's home were shut off, and Ajabu perhaps sensed the oddity. Within a few feet from the house, Ajabu halted for air streams to flow through the nostrils, distinguishing familiar scents, aromas, and that of doom. Every step from then onward was measured.

For extra camouflage, the cage was disguised with the same material as the pen. As it approached the cage, the scent diffusing from the cage was that of a female, so it passed over. The goat pen was its favorite, saliva dripped from its jaws like a faulty faucet, gathering sand as it hit the ground. The rangers were clueless about Ajabu's strange craving: it developed a predilection for billy goats.

Mumbi loved to prepare sumptuous meals and invite close friends over; to this, the rangers could testify. Their eyes were heavy when it mattered most, and the window in the extra room where they waited gave them the best view to shoot or tranquilize. Hurriedly, Ajabu's trailing leg tugged the low-lying cord that triggered a rapid release of the net above that sealed its fate. Not even the terrifying growls of rage were sufficient to set Ajabu free. Soon enough, the lights flicked on, and Jomo burst into his parents' room.

"Baba, we got it!" Jomo yelled.

"Got what?" a startled Gitonga asked.

For a few seconds, the news didn't sink in, but when it did eventually, his legs gained the youthfulness of a sprinter as he darted through the door, leaving Mumbi behind. Her instant reaction was to hide behind the door. The commotion inside rattled the slumbering rangers, and they dashed through the back doors. As a mark of honor, one of the park rangers gave Jomo a tranquilizing gun, and he didn't miss from close range. Ajabu's squealing and violent tussle lasted a brief moment before it became sedated. Jomo hardly remembered what a father's embrace felt like, but he was delighted with this one. To see father and son in an embrace was for Mumbi an utter bliss!

By sunrise, Jaali stood at a distance, watching with keen interest as officials of the Wildlife Conservation took possession of Ajabu, leaving onlookers dumbfounded as it was transported to the zoo. In the coming days, lips wagged across the foothills of Mount Kenya about one mysterious cat, which was a rare occurrence and a reminder of the hidden mysteries of nature. But for the absent few, Ajabu was the legend of the white leopard.

*****

The *mugad* sent for Jomo, and Gitonga's expression was that of bewilderment. Sia welcomed Jomo at the door when he arrived with great delight.

"Welcome, my son," Jaali said.

"Great *mugad*, I greet you," Jomo responded.

"Come with me," Jaali requested.

They retreated to Jaali's divination chambers. Sia's curiosity was not hidden. Like a ballerina, she tiptoed to the door of the chambers and listened.

"My sons, the tradition of our ancestors have served us in times of our need," Jaali said.

Jomo listened with rapt attention.

"What we have must not be lost. We must let our children and those yet unborn glance at the past but look forward to the future."

"Why all these words, *mugad*?" Jomo asked.

Jaali raised his eyebrows. "Patience, my son, patience," he said.

"Chaos is the price you, youths, pay for a life on the fast lane. While we all learned from our elders' mistakes, you all want to make mistakes before learning."

Jomo was uneasy; he cast his mind back and forth, not hoping to hear a guilty verdict.

"We must now record history on the pages of books. Your understanding of animals and plants gives me the confidence to pass on the torch of our ancestors to you," Jaali acknowledged.

Overwhelmed, Jomo tried making sense of what he heard. *I think he must be losing his mind. Even interrupting him could spell calamity. What kind of torch is he talking about?*

"I don't understand what you mean?" Jomo asked.

"Return tomorrow with a notepad. Don't delay!" Jaali demanded.

Mixed feelings were written all over Jomo's face as he departed. Sia slumped to the side of the entrance door before Jomo departed, but a lot was on his mind to notice the motionless eavesdropper. Last thing Sia saw was a flash before it went dim; now, she was groggy after Jaali revived her.

"Save me all that talk, what was this visit about?" Sia asked.

"Is that the reason why you fell?" Jaali asked. "I should have been aware of your theatrics."

Sia was irritable. "Oh, please!" she said.

"I needed to hasten him. Young men of today seem to take time for granted."

"Something doesn't sound right," Sia said in a low tone.

"May I have some food now, please?" Jaali requested.

Within three days, Jomo and Jaali completed the documentation and cataloging of medicinal herbs and their specific uses.

*****

At Gitonga's homestead, work was underway for the modernized animal pen and office building—thanks to the special funds for farmers that Jomo had access to at the Ministry of Wildlife Conservation. Jomo was beginning to overstretch his budget, so he needed to employ extra hands on the farmland. So he sought to cut cost by employing his children—Wangai, Mimi, and Patrick—after all, they were on summer break. On the other hand, Zawadi, his wife, had different plans as a result of the frosty relationship with her in-laws. This was apparent during the construction phase when she chose to party with her bourgeoisie friends in a highbrow Nairobi district.

Wangai, Mimi, and Patrick were hands-on at the farm. Gitonga on occasions would engage them with a few moments of games and riddles. The girls preferred to cook with grandma occasionally, leaving Patrick with his father and grandpa to continue with other construction work.

After a hard day's labor, Gitonga paused to wipe the sweat on his face; he marveled at the transformation. A land that once stood thatched fences, barns, and pens had become a field of new possibilities.

"Son, I am proud of you," Gitonga said as he looked at the ongoing work.

"Thank you, Baba! I am glad you gave your blessings," Jomo replied with a smile.

"Jaali gave you a lot to learn, tell me about it," a curious Gitonga inquired.

"It's about our traditional herbs and their healing powers, the legacy of the *mugad* and the Meru people," Jomo explained.

"Hmm, I wonder why he spoke to you about all these," Gitonga wondered, "but I remember his father went to be with our ancestors after he spoke about the rise of Umoja."

By this time, it occurred to Gitonga that the *mugad's* earlier visit was auspicious. Suddenly, he reached an epiphany! *Ajabu was the spirit from another world that the mugad expressed concerns about.*

Jomo's children loved to play with the little goats, sometimes riding on the backs of calves for fun. Seated on the porch were Jomo, Gitonga, and Mumbi, and the sight of the children getting their hands dirty on the farm was pleasing.

After all the glamour, pleasure trips, and rides, Zawadi felt like a loner whenever she returned to an empty home. It dawned on her the kind of wife, mother, and daughter-in-law she had become. Even a few glasses of cognac on the rocks could not douse the self-guilt that lingered like rain clouds. The next morning, she packed her Louis Vuitton suitcase and headed for Meru. She arrived thirty minutes later to the delight of her children.

"Mom!" the children yelled as they raced toward Zawadi.

"Be nice to her, Gitonga," Mumbi pleaded in a whisper, but he responded with a shrug.

Zawadi knelt down in front of her father-in-law to greet him.

After a slight pause, Mumbi said "Welcome, my child!" and she left to show the kids where to put the suitcase.

From top to bottom, Gitonga looked at Zawadi, then he stretched his hands and patted her shoulders.

*****

Craig arrived with a team of engineers at Meru a week ahead of the scheduled date to hold talks with Jomo and finalize the details of the MOU. Intentionally, Craig held back from visiting Jaali until the following morning.

The fateful morning after Craig arrived in Meru, he headed for Jaali's home but was welcomed with echoes of loud wailing. Meru's great *mugad* had moved on to the great beyond. Craig knew the day it would happen for Jaali spoke of his death with clarity. Sia's inconsolable wailing and the crowd that gathered to pay homage dampened Craig's spirit; he felt the best time to honor his friend was to sign the MOU, and it couldn't come any sooner than now. Prior arrangements were made to sign the MOU officially, but Craig deliberately delayed the process, and now—in the presence of the Kenyan government officials and other stakeholders, the document was signed. G&L Pharmaceutical Africa was born!

Jomo was approached on the farm to accept the new role since he was now the new custodian of the Meru tradition. It was not a difficult decision to make for the farm project was in its final stages. Two days later, the official unveiling of the planned manufacturing plant was attended by well-meaning government officials and the Meru citizens.

Throughout the occasion, Mumbi pouted at two newfound hyenas laughing at the end of their table over a bottle of red wine. She rolled her eyes at Gitonga and Zawadi at their senseless rib-cracking jokes.

"Come here, my boy! Your wife is everyday beautiful," Gitonga complimented Jomo. "When did you develop this eye for good things?" he asked.

Jomo was bewildered and looked at his mother who rose from her seated position.

"Give me that stinking bottle!" she said, snatching the wine. "No more wine for the year!" she insisted.

"But it's not nighttime yet," Gitonga responded.

Mumbi let out a huge sigh and said, "You're looking hopeless right now. Come on, let's go!"

Gitonga staggered as Mumbi tugged his hands. But only as far as his cognition could muster a sentence: The sun still shines on those who wait for the morning to come.

End

WORMS OF BLACK GOLD CREEK

The writer cannot be a mere storyteller...he or she must be actively involved shaping its present and its future.

—Ken Saro-Wiwa

It was Boma Pepple's ninth year working in Luanda, Angola. On this sunny, mid-January afternoon, from the dizzying heights of the twentieth floor, he peered through the sunproof glass windows in his office at Bismarck Oil and Gas (BOG). The impressive tower stood strategically overlooking the coastline. Sights of the coral blue sea, oceanfront, and moving cars from the top were spectacular! Across the road, swaying palm trees on the white, sandy beachfront lined the coastline with precision. Tourists, expatriates, and citizens alike dotted the bay—some jogging along the trail while others suntanned on the beach. The view was a stark contrast from Boma's riverine hometown, Bodo, where the memories of waterways and creeks of the Niger Delta, held a special place in his heart.

Boma pondered over a weeklong correspondence with Mr. Adamu of the National Petroleum Authority of Nigeria (NPAN). It was mouthwatering an offer on paper to reconsider leaving his position as Director of Quality and Environmental Control at BOG. The call to serve his fatherland burned deeply in his heart, but the same land of his birth turned him to a forced migrant, a son banished into obscurity until he became a household name on the pages of newspapers and magazines across the continent. Every passing day was crucial for Boma to accept or decline the opportunity back in

Nigeria—having no more than sixty days to tender his resignation at BOG. Tough choices were not strange to Boma, but this one ostensibly put him in a dilemma. Angola had a special place in his heart; it provided a platform for novelty, expression, and success. The curse of "Black Gold" laid upon Bodo by Shelliburton consigned the people to abject penury. However, the thought of salvaging the community and the wider Ogoniland was a source of motivation to accept the offer. The decision was a no-brainer. Boma picked up the telephone, and Mr. Adamu was on the other end of the call.

"Sir, I have accepted your offer. Expect my acceptance letter via e-mail."

"Mr. Boma, we are certainly delighted to have you on board in May. We shall follow up with proper documents for your perusal and subsequent signatures when we receive your letter," an elated Adamu replied.

Moving back home now wasn't far from his plans, but this offer was a lifetime opportunity, especially if it meant proving a point to Professor George Alaribe who frustrated his ambitions.

*****

Life in Bodo before Boma relocated to Angola moved at sedate pace. The mangrove swamp was all the people knew, and it provided the fishermen and their families' money and food for the many mouths at home. Boma, the first of two children, barely enjoyed his early childhood; of course, not by choice. As a little boy, he would set out fishing in the early hours of the day with his father, Samankwe, the widely revered fisherman whose mastery of the creeks, its tides, and the terrain of the mangrove was out of this world. Some called him "Wizard of the Creek." It was not surprising to see the precocious fisherman in Boma.

As a teenager, Boma's peers often recall a humble lad, but the mangrove and creek transformed him to a showman—often dazzling the young ladies with his brawny definition, unintentionally shaming his peers in the creeks with incredible swimming abilities. If adulations from female admirers were measurable, Boma received them in quantum, and Jaja, his best friend, lived vicariously through him; he could paint a picture so vivid in a way that it became difficult to decipher if they were fables. In fact, Jaja once told listeners that a mermaid bestowed special powers on Boma, alluding to his superior agility and endurance beneath the waters.

There was more to Boma besides fishing and swimming. Samankwe believed the classrooms were a sure escape from the marshy enclaves and had sufficient reserves to send Boma to school. Unfortunately, all that changed in 2008 when one of the worn-out Shelliburton pipelines, like ailing veins, split open, releasing from it thick, black crude that spread across the marshy soils and waters. Life became harsh for the people. The days of women trekking short distances to pick sea snails, periwinkles, oysters, bivalves by the riverbank now took extensive searches with fewer basins to fill up. Boma's father and uncles were subjected to miles of travels to sell their catch. He would sit outside their modest house, counting the stars and listening to the sounds of crickets and croaking toads under the dark skies waiting for his father's return—sometimes as long as two months. Many years ago, the air was sweet and pure, nowadays, the air around was heavy with sulfur dioxide emanating from the thoughtless flaring of natural gas: a by-product of crude oil. Glimmering zinc roofing sheets from the skies now looked rusty as a consequence of acid rains.

Luckily for Samankwe, the modest properties he had acquired before his vertebral fracture, which cut short his fishing days, came in handy. Earnings were set aside for Boma's tertiary education. It was one of Samankwe's many calculated gambles he hoped paid off—and it did! Boma was inching closer to be counted as part of a growing list of graduates of Bodo.

Things looked promising for Boma when Professor George Alaribe, popularly referred to as Prof, of Niger Delta extract was appointed Head of Department (HOD) of Geology. One could not help but notice the Prof's diminutive stature, shiny, bald, head, and indefatigable spirit—never failing to be the center of attraction. Prof never hid his love for his people and the disdain for the federal authorities. Frequent trips to the oil spillage sites with the Prof gave

Boma sufficient exposure, and his quest to find solutions for his people with or without the help of the government of the day burned deeply within.

Occasionally, Boma and the professor took soil samples to document the levels of pollution and to ascertain if the soil incurred more pollutants. Halfway through his postgraduate studies in Environmental Geology, Boma discovered something serendipitous. He noticed that an ample amount of indigenous specie of earthworms, *Nsukkadrilus mbae*, invaded the soil sample gathered from the previous expedition in the green room. After testing the levels of hydrocarbons and comparing it to previous soil samples, what he found was astonishing! The previous level of hydrocarbons in the soil was reduced by twenty units compared to its original reading—significantly less than the most recent sample. *Eureka! I could use this to form the basis of my postgraduate thesis,* he thought to himself.

Before 8:00 a.m. the following day, he was seated at the waiting area of the Prof's office. The Prof was at his office exactly 9:00 a.m.

"Young man, what brings you early today?" the professor asked. "Aren't we supposed to meet next week?"

"Sir, this can't wait," Boma replied.

The professor looked at his secretary, Mrs. Margaret Dike, and said, "Make sure no one bothers me for the next hour."

Boma followed behind the Prof; then the professor signaled for him to sit down. "So, tell me, what is it that can't wait?"

"Sir, we could be up to something here!" He spoke with enthusiasm, but the professor was unmoved.

Boma went straight to the crux of the matter. "Yesterday evening, I decided to run a test of the samples we collected at Bodo months ago," he said, "just to compare the levels of the aromatic hydrocarbons in the soil."

The professor adjusted his posture. "Go on," he demanded.

"Now, the levels of the aromatic hydrocarbons dropped twenty units compared to the most recent sample."

"How is this possible?" the professor asked.

An exuberant Boma explained, "I am almost convinced that the worms, *Nsukkadrilus mbae*, played a major role."

Visibly impatient, the professor retorted, "Look, young man, I don't have time for skullduggery."

"Prof, I can run another sample to test this finding," Boma pleaded, "and if indeed the result is accurate, we can overlook the government and seek private funding."

"We must not get ahead of ourselves," the professor cautioned. "Rerun the test as you have suggested and get back to me as soon as possible."

"Surely, Prof, I shall be back with it." And Boma was quick through the doors.

Prof thought long and hard about this prospect for a couple of minutes and imagined the thoughts of new beginnings and possibly having a shot as a consultant for the federal government. These were early days, and the Prof wasn't the type to get ahead of himself, and so he went about his daily office routines.

Twenty-four hours later, Boma repeated the tests, and the aromatic hydrocarbons depleted even further. Boma knew that this was an opportunity too good to pass; besides, he was one to make an impression. Next, he entered the data into a spreadsheet and got inspired, creating pie charts, histograms, etc.

The following day, the Prof paced around his office, reading through the startling report. He stopped to glance at the unassuming, smart aleck seated in his office. Written in these reports were key clues for a novel idea in Environmental Geology; but to him, Boma was not ripe for the limelight, considering the number of years most academics spend building relevance. It would have been impressive for the Prof had he discovered this novel idea. All the bald and gray hair he flaunted, generally associated with academic prowess, came to naught. Indeed, cerebral mileage, which the Prof had in leaps and bounds, wasn't inextricably linked to age, innovation, nor inspiration; the latter flows from the vault of timeless wisdom decoded by those who are aware.

A weeklong midsemester break was already halfway through, and it came in handy for Boma and his colleagues in the department to focus on the upcoming poster presentation. Prior to this break, Boma had settled in on this project for his thesis and was approved by the Prof. Although Boma put in most of the work, Prof was a valuable resource, providing a body of work on bioremediation and crude oil contaminants for reference.

In recent times, the Department of Geology's prestige and exposure gained reputation in the wider academic community. International firms scouted for the top three graduating candidates from the department. As a result, this project meant a lot to Boma, and the Prof knew that.

*****

The federal government of the day was elected against the backdrop of probity and accountability. True to their words, for once in decades, wide-sweeping changes shook every facet of the polity. Prompted by the Minister of Petroleum and Energy, vice chancellors from three institutions—with geology and environmental backgrounds—were asked to nominate a candidate each for a position: University of Nigeria (UNN), Ahmadu Bello University (ABU), and University of Ibadan (UI). Of the three, Prof was not only the most qualified but also was of Niger Delta origin. Two weeks later, Prof was appointed the Chairman of the Niger Delta Emergency and Relief Trust Fund (NDERTF) whose oversight function borders on matters of environmental disaster and restoration, evacuation, monetary compensation, and more.

News had spread round campus of Prof's federal appointment. His repugnant Napoleon complex shone through as he was adamant about maintaining his position as the HOD. Predictably, access to the Prof was infrequent. Boma noticed the Prof's fervor wane by the day; this saddened the young man. The last trip with the Prof to Bodo was sinister.

While Boma walked passed the trail to the waterfront overlooking the mangrove swamp, he saw Prof from a distance in the company of a band of menacing youths. Conversations were held in cautious tones as some glanced at any instance of a human presence. Boma's gut feeling was to follow along, which he did. Before the Prof and the men disappeared from view, they veered off in the direction of a community hall. As he closed in on them, he could hear the Prof negotiating a substantial amount of slush funds from the NDERTF earmarked by the government for the quarterly stipend meant for the local fishermen, farmers, and their families. Boma heard the conversations that transpired.

PROF. Chief Festus, you know as we do, scratch my back and we'll play ball.

CHIEF. Prof, our people need the money to compensate them.

PROF. Well, they aren't complaining after we built them a water-processing plant.

CHIEF. That's not enough, you should do more.

PROF. Free money comes once in a lifetime. Tell me when last you changed your car?

CHIEF. It's broken down.

PROF. I thought as much! Get rid of it.

CHIEF. No, I can't. It's my only car.

PROF. Chief, if I build a small-scale oil refinery here, you would have this key for a new jeep.

CHIEF. Let me think about it.

PROF. While you think about it, here's $100,000 as welfare package…

Who would have thought that the Prof's life would change in so short a time? Long were the days where the appearance of this erudite son of Bodo bore the look of hardship. Feet that hosted worn-out shoes, graced with red-earth dust, now smiled with pristine leather, well-fitted Armani suits, replacing formless ones. Days of breathlessness from pushing his Peugeot station wagon to jump-start were also gone. Now the customized black Range Rover Sports and BMW 5 Series were welcomed reliefs.

*****

Boma was in Bodo for the weekend before the midsemester break was over. Samankwe, his father, had just finished a gourd of palm wine after a sumptuous meal of spicy tilapia fish, chopped onions and tomatoes, a side of green vegetables as Boma walked in from the gates. He greeted his father and attempted to walk past him with a 50 lbs. worth of crude oil-laden soil in a sturdy, plastic receptacle the size of stowaway bin.

The weight of Samankwe's deep thoughts seemed to lower his head. "My son," he said.

"Yes, Dad," Boma replied.

Samankwe raised his head, and Boma knew what was obtainable from the tone of his voice.

"I have heard on good authority that you plan to criticize your HOD to his hearing," he said, reclining. Boma was careful not to interrupt his father as he continued, "For whatever reason it is, do not allow the exuberance of your youth stir you away from the big picture."

The young man was eager to respond, but Samankwe motioned, then, he (Boma) held back.

"I no longer possess the bones of my youth, neither do I have the strength of a wild horse. Our elders say, what the dog saw and barked ferociously, the sheep saw the same thing and turned a blind eye to it."

"How do you mean, Father?"

"Under these skies," his father said, pointing upward, "there's a set day for reckoning." Then he concluded, "Let the professor conduct himself as he pleases."

Boma was surprised to hear his father's position but was quick to respond, "We can't allow our kinsman betray us."

Samankwe stared at his son briefly then continued to drink the palm wine. The lull was suggestive; Boma departed his father's presence and headed for his room.

Behind Samankwe, a lanky frame tiptoed past him: it was Tega, Boma's younger sister. She was eavesdropping all the while, and as soon as Boma retired to his room, she sneaked right behind. Tega was fond of her big brother. Growing up with her brother was adventurous and fun-filled; it offered her stints of capricious swimming lessons and fishing expeditions, which exasperated their mother, Belema. Like her brother, she learned to climb mango and coconut trees—Boma often bragged about his sister's boyish displays. Whenever Boma was told to scale large bales of fish alone as punishment for taking his sister out to swim, he would toss a few to Tega to roast secretly. Fish-scaling was a chore Boma detested, but his sister's connivance brought delight. Belema never caught up on their shenanigans until much later.

Inside his room now, she asked, "Why do you look dejected?"

"Do I look it?" Boma replied.

Tega stood akimbo with a smirk on her face and said, "I can figure you out with my eyes closed." She continued after a slight pause, "Tell me more about this whole saga of your experiment and the Prof."

Boma sighed. "Not now, Tega."

"Look, sulking never solved a problem, so you better start talking," she insisted.

Such was Tega's power of persuasion that it injected some life into him, and soon enough he sat up.

"Well, see that box over there," he said, pointing to the corner of the room, "it contains soil samples from Bodo's mangrove swamp."

She squinted as if to suggest she was lost amid his scholastic light. "Ah, Boma! These descriptions are heavy to comprehend," she said, "please, explain."

"That container has a sample of crude oil-laden soil with earthworms," he said, sounding beleaguered.

"So what has this got to do with the Prof?" she asked.

"We both had the vision of restoring our once fertile soil, independent of the federal government's help," he said. "Our people deserve a better life."

Tega allowed him flow uninterrupted; at least, that was the barest minimum she could offer him. At an instant, his voice sounded like the ghost of one of the fallen Ogoni Nine heroes, Ken Saro-Wiwa—the feeling was uncanny.

"Beneath our soil is our collective wealth," he said, fuming. "The lifeline of the nation hemorrhages crude oil from fractured pipelines."

Tega interjected, "I am still waiting to get an answer to my initial question."

"The Prof has tampered with funds from the NDERTF!" he said, gesticulating.

"How sure are you?" Tega cautiously asked.

Boma was quite irritable. "Maybe you are from another community for not seeing his new country home and brand-new cars," he said. "I gather the Prof is now into illegal bunkering."

Tega was shocked. "This is unbelievable!" she said.

Boma's vituperations were necessary to blow off steam. Tega watched his countenance briefly and drew his attention to their father's words. She was very practical in matters of life and expressed her concerns regarding Boma's outspoken nature toward the Prof's sharp practices.

"Boma, stay clear from his shenanigans and concentrate on finishing your postgraduate studies," Tega implored. "Afterward, you can set up your own company and be of help."

Even though Boma nodded in the affirmative in response to her suggestion, she didn't see it as convincing because he never wavered. Nevertheless, the night was still young and tranquil for Tega to treat her brother to some freshly roasted yellow corn and African pear. Both had their fill and retired about 9:00 p.m. for the night because Boma had to set out very early in the morning to avoid unfavorable weather conditions that could compromise his sample experiment.

Morning arrived, but the sun still slumbered. Samankwe and his household bade their son farewell as he departed. Boma could recall a number of speedboat rides, but this one was unpleasant. With one hand on the wheels and the other on a bright lamp, the seaman glided through the creeks like a water skater, cutting through the waterways with an air of steady recklessness. Boma held on as the boat swerved. Splashing sounds of the parting waters petrified him, but the cool vapors that settled on his skin brought temporal calm. In a matter of minutes, he arrived at the motor park where he chartered a taxi en route to Enugu.

*****

Classes resumed on campus the Monday after the midsemester break, and poster presentations were due four weeks later. April showers came as a timely relief. For Boma, it was incumbent upon him to take the next step toward the pilot trial. With the help of young locals, he paid twenty Naira apiece to collect a substantial amount of *Nsukkadrilus mbae*. The worms weighed 10 lbs. and were added to the previously harvested soil, then, mulch was added for nutrients before sealing it with an aerated lid. Halfway through the third week, preliminary findings were recorded.

The penultimate week before the poster presentation, the Prof summoned Boma, and the timing was rather odd for Boma considering the fact that the Prof became indifferent since assuming the leadership of NDERTF. He arrived at the Prof's office on his way to the laboratory. Just walking out of the Prof's office was Professor Olívio dos Santos from the Agostinho Neto University, Luanda, Angola. He arrived as an exchange professor for the semester and was part of the review panel for the poster presentations. Boma could tell from a distance that the bespectacled man of average height was an academic by virtue of his wild, grayish-black hair and beard.

Prof asked for updates on the ongoing experiment, but Boma was naive to think that his novel idea was a welcomed one. To make matters worse, Boma's goof proved a costly one. He was compelled to make known the sighting of the Prof in company of the village chief. Had he refrained from reminding the Prof to work for the people now that he was in the position, things would have fizzled off naturally.

"Get out of my office!" the professor yelled.

Boma tried to show remorse, but it was too late now. When Boma left, the Prof called his secretary and directed her to strike his name from the poster presentation.

On the departmental list, Boma knew his name always came last, which meant that his poster presentation was to be heard last. The last candidate finished presenting in the conference room, and Boma walked up to the department secretary (Mrs. Margaret) who took hold of a copy of the presentation; embarrassingly, his name was omitted. He fussed, and tempers rose to boiling point.

She comforted him with the words "Every disappointment is a blessing…" but those words fell on deaf ears.

"Ma'am, please, I don't want to hear that!" Boma said with vexation.

"Only the HOD knows the reason," Margaret said.

"Who?" he asked with bloodshot eyes.

"Ah! You didn't hear it from me, please, oh," she said after recognizing her slipup.

"Why do the mighty get away with heavy-handedness?" he asked loudly.

While the secretary tried to pacify Boma, Professor Olívio dos Santos stepped out of the conference room for a restroom break. On his way back, he could not help but notice Boma's frustration and bickering.

Professor Santos inquired, "May I ask what the matter is?"

Boma took deep breaths, feeling bitter and betrayed. "Sir, my name was removed from the list without reason," he said. "This is unfair and unjust!"

"Are you sure about this?" the professor asked Boma. He glanced at the secretary, seeking confirmation of the claims.

"Let me have the hardcopy of the presentation," the professor requested.

From what transpired, as Boma would learn a few days later, Prof cast aspersions on Boma's body of work, citing lack of integrity and originality as prime reasons. Professor dos Santos had seen a few cases of parochialism in his thirty odd years in the academia across the continent, so he made Boma's case a priority.

Boma was left in limbo as to what next to do following his academic probation. In a turn of events, Professor dos Santos presented Boma an acceptance letter to complete his degree at the Agostinho Neto University with a full scholarship and an option of working with BOG upon graduation. Overwhelmed with joy unspeakable, Boma dropped to his knees with emphatic gratitude! The rest they say belongs to history…

*****

In present times, the last phase of the five-year oil spill cleanup at Cabinda neared completion. Beyond any stretch of the imagination, Boma, the little boy of Bodo, could not have conceived the grand plan of the Lord of times and seasons, infinite in all His ways, boundless in miracles. Who would have imagined combining the role of a postgraduate and lead expatriate petroleum geologist? With a talent like his, BOG secured his services before graduation.

Boma ran a thorough Geographical Information System analysis over a five-mile stretch, north to south of the coastline. The ground penetrating radars and aerial photos provided an estimate of the surface area and depth of polluted soil. The scope of the contamination required precision, above all, expertise which Boma had in excess. From experience, he knew that partial evacuation of crude oil-laden soil in addition to unforeseen geological conditions was potentially hazardous, if not now, sometime in the near future. Thus, he utilized the advantage of sinking boreholes to loosen up the soil to introduce solvents that break down benzene, toluene, and other hydrocarbons. After a month, *Nsukkadrilus mbae* would then be introduced into the pretreated soil with a mixture of brewery marsh, wood chips, and grass for another four weeks to eliminate recalcitrant hydrocarbons and regenerate the soil nutrients.

Early January 2009, just before Boma left his office, he received an e-mail notification from Alhaji Adamu with a formal offer letter attached to it. Finally, it was time to banish those haunting thoughts of his forced migration. Returning home was not the issue, the prime concern was Isabella, his girlfriend of two years. She heard a great deal about Nigeria, some good and, most of the other reports, overwhelmingly negative. Thankfully, Boma's enduring sentiments for Nigeria, above all, Bodo, was reassuring.

*****

Getting along with Isabella was seamless because she was well travelled; as a matter of fact, she established an NGO in Cabinda that catered to victims of oil spillage. Born into an affluent family and the first of three children, Isabella's childhood taught her that the soul of family thrives on love and sacrifice even if it meant moving to places unknown. She was no stranger to this. As a prominent politician under the then President of Angola, Agostinho Neto, her father served as ambassador to the United Nations, as well as Ghana. Wherever the family was transferred, her mother, a nurse, made it a home.

Friday was a day to relax, but Boma pondered about how best to make known his proposal to Isabella who was due to arrive the next day from a disaster relief mission in Maputo, Mozambique. As soon as she arrived, she spotted Boma's waiting car.

When preparedness mattered, Boma had it in substantial measure, but his subconscious mind shrunk his poise. His emotion-stuck lips prevented him from following through on well-rehearsed proposal lines.

"Love, did you, folks, have a lot of displaced people since the last one seven years ago?"

She sighed, running her fingers through her curly hair. "Sweetie, don't even remind me," she said with animation. "The government had better build more dams quickly or else future Zambezi valley flooding will be frightening."

"Worse than the previous one I suppose," he assumed.

"Such a tragedy to see young orphans, elderly men and women helpless," she said in a disapproving manner.

There was stillness for a moment, so Boma looked to the side and noticed Isabella dozing off and slightly nodding.

"Darling," he said, "I'd like to share something with you." He paused to see her reaction to determine if he'd proceed with the conversation or wait until another opportunity presents itself.

"Yes, honey, what's on your mind?" she asked.

There was just something about Isabella's immaculate, hazel eyes that snuffed out Boma's confidence each time he tried to be serious.

Overcome by anxiety, he suggested, "I think you should nap 'coz it can wait."

She looked at him then folded her arms waiting for a word. Boma was now compelled to speak.

"I accepted an offer from the National Petroleum Authority of Nigeria," he said, "and I want to know if you would relocate with me?"

Surprised, she asked, "To Nigeria?" Boma nodded in the affirmative.

It was a difficult question posed to Isabella, and he was unsure of her reaction. Until they arrived at his home, she uttered no words. The cook had prepared a tasty staple meal of Fish *calulu* and *funge*, which they ate, talking lightheartedly, before retiring for the night.

Very early on Monday morning, while Boma still snored like a tractor running low on engine oil, Isabella was ready to leave for work. She tapped him, and he shuddered.

"When do we leave for Nigeria?" she asked.

Boma was shocked and sleep soon eluded him. "The first Saturday in May."

"Roughly seventy odd days from today," she said. "Let's have a detailed conversation later today."

"Are you not scared to relocate?" he asked.

"For the man that completes me," she said, "it's worth the move."

The statement that endeared him to her was profound.

"My mortality is borderless, and my heart is your home," she said. "You have my heart, and if it meant the world to you, I'm certain it's yours to lose."

*****

Bodo and the neighboring communities, at least by historical antecedents, were relatively peaceful; moreover, in recent times, a new and terrible menace began to emerge. Pipeline vandalization, kidnapping, and illegal crude oil bunkering grounded the economy to a halt. It came as no surprise to keen observers of the region.

Past government's gross dereliction of duty pushed these peace-loving communities, as a consequence, to the brink of annihilation. Environmental degradation, joblessness, and youth restiveness had become a cost too heavy to bear. Apprehension swept through the land as gun-wielding boats swerve through the creeks like nocturnal marauders seeking for unfortunate victims. Freeing kidnapped expatriates with colossal ransoms served idle youths more than a dose of adrenaline rush. In secret enclaves of the creeks, shattered pipelines were a constant source of crude oil that fed vast networks of mushroom refineries like cancer cells.

Prof was at the height of illegal crude oil bunkering, sliding past a retinue of naval patrol team with an armada of ships and barges in the dead of the nights. Shamefully, the Prof who was touted to be the next recognizable, uncompromising patriot since the demise of the "Ogoni Martyrs" some fifteen years ago was now an object of public lampoon.

Mass media reports, both foreign and local, lambasted the federal government without ceasing. They accused the government for its lackluster attitude toward a people on whose land the country is sustained.

At the center of this debacle, Shelliburton Oil Company received most of the backlash. Since it began oil exploration in the late 1950s, not one single pipeline was maintained, causing inevitable breaks and leakages. Relentless public outcries to the authorities on the spillage were treated with kid gloves. Before anyone could respond, the environmental pollution was now beyond containment. Bodo and the wider Ogoniland have become derelict.

*****

Previous governments resorted to militarization by way of securing the oil facilities, but the current administration of President Panshak Isaac focused on the root cause; his actions had to be decisive. Previous recommendations relating to the unrest amounted to naught—an ocean of ink on a forest of papers.

An advance party of emissaries waited to welcome the president. The president, after careful introspection, flipped the script of protocols, opting to speak randomly to vulnerable residents in Bodo.

Despite the Prof's diversion tactics, the president turned in the direction of Samankwe's house. Sweat drops trickled down from the side of the Prof's head to the chin. The entourage stopped a few feet away while the Prof went into the house to inform Samankwe of the arrival of the number one citizen. Upon gaining entry, he met Belema and saw Tega looking outside from the window. It didn't take more than a minute for mother and daughter to figure out why the Prof was at their household: simply to hoodwink the president.

"Ah! Madam, the president is here," he said, "don't forget to put in a good word for me as he has heard nice things about your family."

"Prof, I don't understand your point," she replied.

Tega interjected, "Prof, my brother's career could have been over because of you—"

She was still talking when the Prof interrupted, "Young lady, this is not the time for this."

Some of the responses from Belema and Tega to the Prof could have been spoken at a cordial pitch, but their amplified voices attracted attention. Before he could hush them both, the president stepped into the house to find out the cause of the raucous exchanges. Only the president's look caused the Prof to stutter. "Nothing, sir…I mean, Your Excellency."

Tega was ready to take the family's pound of flesh. "Your Excellency, he has failed our people."

"Sir, she must be mistaken," the Prof refuted with trepidations. "Is your father not at home?"

Incidentally, Samankwe was fast asleep when all this transpired but heard later about the visit.

The president ordered his chief of staff to determine the root of the family's grievance, then he departed with his entourage. For the remainder of the trip, the president appeared lighthearted with his staff but shared little on his impression of the tour; nevertheless, beneath the veil, sadness for the lack of urgency on the part of government pierced his heart.

*****

On the Cabinda, Luanda Site Project, the measurements of hydrocarbons were favorable, and BOG was unprepared for the news that broke from local online media captioned THE TRAITOR WITHIN BOG.

Isabella broke the news feed to Boma while he was attending to the penultimate data analysis of the final cleanup. It wasn't the news he had hoped to hear, but he masked his emotions until the close of the day.

On his ride home, his phone rang. It was the company's secretary asking him to be present at a panel of inquiry. The meeting was ill-timed for his job was at stake. When the meeting of inquiry ended, Björn Andersøn, the CEO, called him to the side.

"Boma, I thought we had a good relationship?" he asked. "But I don't want to stand in your way…"

"It was my intention to let you know before I tender my resignation," Boma replied.

"My hands are tied, but we must make this a seamless transition between us," Andersøn said with understanding.

"I'll have my resignation letter at your desk tomorrow," Boma assured him.

"Best of luck, my friend!" Andersøn said then shook his hands and departed.

*****

Mr. Babayaro's shady deals at the NPAN was protected in the past by his protégé, Alhaji Adamu. As the organization's general manager (GM), his successes were by and large a function of his loyal deputy. In recent times, their relationship had become frosty since Adamu refused to marry his eldest daughter; instead, he chose to marry his longtime Eritrean sweetheart, Samira Abdelazeez. The pair met when Adamu was at the Delft University of Technology, Netherlands.

Adamu was a man of integrity: cerebral by nature, as well as innovative. Lasting changes made at the organization were solely his ideas but the glory taken by his estranged boss. As a matter of fact, recruiting Boma was principally Adamu's idea because he felt the organization needed to create a department that worked in tandem with oil exploration companies to prevent water and land pollution.

Upon the president's return at the State House Villa, he dispatched a letter to the senate president requesting the upper house to act on a number of pressing issues regarding the petroleum sector, Shelliburton's oil spillage, and that of the NDERTF. Some of the findings of the petitions from the past that the senate ad hoc committee on petroleum affairs revisited were startling! The committee discovered that since the arrival of Shelliburton to Bodo community—and part of the wider Ogoniland—in 1958, a quarter of a million barrels spilled into the wetlands owing to the lack of maintenance of pipelines. Between 2008 and 2009, two fifty-five-year-old pipelines fractured and spilled an estimated half a million barrels into the creeks and mangroves, destroying farmlands and rivers, ultimately destroying their sources of livelihood. The committee also looked into the pending lawsuits levied against Shelliburton by the people of Bodo Community at a British court. Sadly, children born recently in the Bodo and the surrounding Ogoniland have several public health issues: sinusitis, bronchitis, cancer, and asthma have all been on the rise.

The senate ad hoc committee set out on a two-day working tour of Ogoniland. Heavily guarded by a detachment of mobile police escorts, the committee members traversed 404 square miles of Ogoniland on speedboats. Bodo community was particularly of interest because it was one of the most affected. As they closed in within a mile, black-colored oil sheen floated atop the water surface. To the sides of the mazy mangrove swamps, dark fumes rose as if to protest against the presence of the unwelcomed visitors, releasing noxious fumes as they covered their noses from the putrid smell of the swamps. Upstream, bare-chested fishermen hurled insults at men accosted by a team from the Navy and Civil Defense Corps. *What must have been the cause?* the members thought. The fishermen's grouse were simple: the Prof caused more damage to the land with his illegal oil bunkering. The Prof, as the committee learned, owned and controlled the most sophisticated maritime barges—each costing six million Naira—with a distribution ring a notch above the rest. Before the committee members left the scene, the illegal refineries were pulverized with sophisticated explosives.

Following the allegations of the men accosted, the Nigerian customs tracked the barges and were hot on their trail.

As they reached Bodo community, it was clear that the effect of crude oil spillage was devastating. Roots from the mangrove that jotted out at low tide served as gatekeepers of free-floating crude oil, giving the roots a greasy coat. Tattered clothes swung wherever the wind blew while the ponds that once held the fishermen's game have become a poisoned chalice for the fishes.

The next day after the tour, the committee visited oil installations and pipelines of the entire Ogoniland before their airlifting to Port-Harcourt en route Abuja.

*****

Prof's realization of the possibility of an indictment troubled him. Above all, he had lost favor with his kinsmen and made so many enemies back at the university. Mr. Babayaro's office was responsible for funding the NDERTF, and so it was little wonder why the Prof and Babayaro covered their tracks.

March 2009 was rife with expectations for the country, but as the displeasure among the citizens was mounting by the day, crude oil revenue was at an all-time low because of pipeline vandalization and explosions. Babayaro had several meetings with the Prof, but this particular meeting was bugged.

"'Yaro, my friend, the cargo we shipped to Porto-Novo has arrived," the Prof said.

"I hope they don't ask stupid questions?" Babayaro asked.

"You know that scalawag of a custom comptroller was beginning to make trouble," he said, "but we 'watered' his palms."

"How soon will the wire transfer come through?" he asked.

"You should receive an alert of five million dollars before nightfall," the Prof said with enthusiasm.

"*Nagode* (thank you), Prof," Babayaro said. "But we are good before the next federal allocation, right?" he asked.

53

"Yes, two more barges should be on the way in a fortnight," the Prof assured. "One should be leaving Cotonou for Abidjan and the other to Lomé."

"We can tell the boys to stop the explosions till further notice," Babayaro suggested.

The Prof responded emphatically, "Roger that, boss!"

*****

Courage eluded Boma to propose to Isabella the day she returned from Maputo. He had the ring in his house but contended with the feeling of not trying to coerce her into moving back to Nigeria with him. It had to be a decision that was personal and free of attachments to an engagement. She had to agree to it wholeheartedly. Surprisingly, everything worked itself out, but Boma tarried for a while with the decision.

Boma confided in Tega about the proposal, and she was supportive because she had become fond of Isabella for over two years—a sort of big sister to little sister relationship. Tega was not sure how her parents would react, but she encouraged her brother to secure their parents' blessing. Boma placed a call at the time Tega was in their parents' midst.

"Ah! My director," as Boma was now fondly called by his father, "*wetin* dey happen?" he asked.

"Papa, nothing much o!" replied Boma.

Boma's father asked lightheartedly in a manner soliciting for a gift, "Any better?"

Then Boma laughed at the side joke and took advantage of the lively mood.

"Papa, please, put the phone on speaker if Mama is there," he requested. "I have something to tell you both."

"We are listening," both parents replied.

"You remember Isabella?" he asked.

"Your friend?" his father asked. "Go on..."

"I have decided to marry her," he said. "I want to propose to her."

A pin-dropped silence ensued for about two minutes. His mother let out a sigh while his father looked over to his sister and back at his wife.

"Are you sure about this?" he asked Boma.

"We give you our blessings," his father said. "May it go well with you as you have never brought us shame."

His sister was dancing at the corner of the living room to the amazement of her parents.

Boma concluded, "If she agrees, we'll be back to Nigeria for good first week in May."

Isabella arrived at Boma's house on a Saturday morning. He relieved his domestic staff from their duties earlier in the day. She had the spare key to the entrance, so she made her way to the living room. Boma was seated quietly at the dining table when he heard her yell his name. Isabella was surprised that he was not watching his regular European league football game (soccer as some would say). Thirsty, she made her way to the kitchen but was surprised to see the table well dressed in Victorian style.

"All these for a breakfast, love?" Isabella asked.

"Morning, sunshine!" he greeted warmly. "Come have a seat."

"Sorry, honey, my manners are questionable this morning. How do you know that I am so hungry?" she asked.

"Thought I should appreciate Mrs. Pepple."

"Ah! Talk is cheap," she said as she went in on the food.

It didn't sink in until a few minutes. "Wait a minute, what did you just call me?" she asked.

"Exactly what you heard." Boma winked.

Breakfast was done, but all through the conversation, she pretended to focus on the many jokes they both shared. She kept waiting to see if Boma will make a formal declaration of his intent to marry her but was disappointed. So she packed up the dishes and walked off to the kitchen gloomy.

Boma played a fast one on me. Foolish me! I hope I have not wasted my time. How stupid could I have been to pack up and leave for a place I know not? Lord, tell me if this is meant to be, Isabella prayed.

Sounds of glassware clanked in the sink in a fit of frustration. Quietly, Boma sneaked up and wrapped his hands around her waist from behind. He kissed her long neck and turned her around, slipped his right hand in his right pocket, and brought out an eighteen-karat diamond engagement ring.

"Darling, would you marry me?" he asked as her eyes welled up with tears.

"Yes!" she affirmed, hugging him tightly and crying like a baby on his shoulders.

"It's okay, Isabella," he said, looking at her with assurance.

The rest of the day was one of ecstasy for Isabella while Boma watched her flurry of emotions with glee. Between letting her family in on the engagement and Boma securing his soon-to-be in-laws' blessings, Isabella was concluding plans to secure a property with an agency back in Port-Harcourt. Meanwhile, she immersed herself in a plethora of information, seeking understanding of an anticipated life in Nigeria. At the center of it all was a lifetime commitment to the vulnerable: the voiceless people of the world.

*****

Boma and Isabella arrived at the Nnamdi Azikwe International Airport, Abuja. A chauffeur was waiting for them who led them to Adamu at the arrival lounge.

"Welcome, Boma!" Adamu said. "Finally, we get to meet."

"Mr. Adamu, very pleased to meet you," he replied. "By the way meet my fiancée, Isabella."

"Wow! She's a beauty," he complemented. "Let me guess, you're Angolan, right?"

"Thanks, Mr. Adamu," she responded with a heartfelt smile. "Yes, a very good guess."

Adamu reached for his pocket in his purple flowing kaftan and handed Boma two round trip tickets to and from Port-Harcourt. Boma's next intention was to see his parents who he had not seen in over eight years and also to introduce his fiancée to them.

They walked through the departure gate in company of Adamu.

"See you soon and enjoy your flight," Adamu said before departing.

Isabella expressed her gratitude, placing her right palm across her chest. "Thanks, Mr. Adamu, you've been so kind."

A modest Adamu responded, "Please, don't give me all the credit," he said, "but thanks indeed."

Forty-five minutes of travel time felt like a blink of an eye as they touched down at Port-Harcourt International Airport at 4:00 p.m. Tega was on hand to receive them. Isabella spotted her first, and both embraced like lost sisters, leaving out Boma. He was pleased to see the two finally meet.

"Sorry, big bro!" she said laughing. "Welcome home!"

"Thanks!" he said. "What of Mom and Dad?"

"Waiting for you both," she replied. "Let's get going, the taxi is hired."

The jolly ride to Ogoniland was about twenty-five miles long. Isabella moved in and out of conversation, soaking up the green scenery with utmost curiosity. Roadside vendors roasting corn, automobile mechanics housed in ramshackle buildings, high-rise buildings and commendable road networks reminded her of Luanda. *We aren't different after all, one family...one human race,* she pondered. All the stories she heard and the hour-long research was a totally different feeling from what stared her in the face. As they mounted the speedboat, Isabella clung onto Tega. For show, the seaman maneuvered the boat, sometimes leaving Isabella dizzy. Boma laughed at her shock while his sister cautioned the seaman.

Arriving Bodo community was humbling. Like Cabinda, the resource that lay beneath the earth was more of a curse than a blessing. Bodo, unlike Cabinda, however, experienced more environmental degradation on a level quite frightening! Isabella's heart sank, and it wasn't surprising when she began to cry, imagining the public health implications stacked against the ordinary man. Tega was magnanimous with her empathy, hugging and reassuring Isabella. Boma was at the front with the seaman, laughing about old tales and catching up on the new things. By the time they disembarked, Isabella was in a better mood.

Boma's parents were seated at the front porch in eager anticipation for Boma and their soon-to-be daughter in-law. Belema was the first to leave her seat, longing for her son's embrace.

"Mom, so nice to see you again!" an excited Boma said.

"My son," Belema repeated three times before hugging him.

Samankwe also immersed himself in the embrace. "My son," he said, "you are welcome!"

"Thank you, Father!"

Before Boma could start the introduction, Belema was quick to it. She winked at Tega then nudged and tugged her to the side.

She held Isabella's hands and guided her to turn around as she observed her figure-hugging blue jeans and well-fitted white T-shirt, looked her up and down, and said, "No wonder my son never bothered to come back. My daughter, these hips can handle at least five grandchildren," she said jokingly, and Isabella laughed warmly, thanking her in her usual manner.

"Ah-ah, are you all right?" Belema asked with a surprised look.

Tega laughed. "No, Mom, she is just thanking you from her heart."

Belema bonded quickly with Isabella, holding her hands to admire her expressive eyes, touching her curly, black hair that had a permanent shine to it. After settling in to the lighthearted conversation, Tega headed for the kitchen to prepare supper, and Isabella followed when she knew it was going to be pounded yam, waterleaf soup with periwinkles—just the opportunity she hoped for to showcase her cooking skills.

Belema was witty to suggest. "Tega, please, keep Isabella from the fire," she said. "Her skin is too soft for that kind of heat."

*****

Weeks after Boma's arrival, the auditor general's report on NPAN was handed to the president. In a confidential package, a copy of the findings was dispatched to Babayaro, but Adamu was on hand to receive it. He opened the report and went through the executive summary, as well as key findings—especially as it relates to

NDERTF. Page by page, he perused the findings and discovered that the extra $15M allocated for the NDERTF supplementary spending was flagged. He knew then that the signs were ominous for his boss. Quickly, he called Babayaro.

"Boss, how close are you to the office?" he asked.

"The driver just pulled in," his boss responded. "Anything the matter?"

"When you get to the office, boss, it's pretty urgent."

Babayaro paced the room before sitting down, but not a clue came to mind to solve this problem. As an afterthought, Adamu reminded Babayaro that their new hire, Boma, was due to resume the following week. A light bulb flickered in his mind to present Boma as a marquee candidate in response to the president's initiative for A Better Niger-Delta in order to save his job.

Before Babayaro could set up a meeting, he was suspended indefinitely from his position as the general manager while Adamu replaced him in an acting capacity. Adamu impressed upon Boma to resume earlier than his start date with a cash advance bonus as compensation. The next day, Boma arrived at Adamu's office only to learn of the shocking revelations of misappropriation by the NDERTF chairman.

"Over to you, Boma," he said, handing over the auditor's report. "The chairman's office is within your purview, and he is your kinsman."

Boma received the report and left for his office to ponder over all he heard. Boma transmitted a letter of invitation via courier with the name Mr. Tonye Clark. The Prof arrived at Boma's office two days later. After both had a cordial meeting and an assurance of each other's support, an elated Prof stood up to leave.

On his way out, Boma said, "Prof, I am Boma Pepple. My secretary has your termination letter and the senate's ad hoc committee summon."

The Prof's heart stopped beating for a moment, wishing the ground would swallow him. He regained composure and stormed out of the office while Boma watched with delight.

*****

In company of Belema and Tega, Isabella visited the neighboring communities devastated by the oil spill. She felt pained by the extent of the devastation and the negative human impact. It was so troubling that she threw up several times amid a river of tears. Ideas concerning her proposed NGO project—which would cater to the plight of Bodo community—ran through her mind. Isabella, Belema and Tega began to brainstorm.

*****

Still smarting from his dismissal as chairman of NDERTF, he received a notification from one of his foot soldiers regarding his last refinery that was razed to the ground by the Nigerian Air Force on routine flight patrol. He was devastated because he sank in over $500,000 in the illegal refinery business, estimating a return on investment worth ten times the initial capital.

A group of Department of State Service's security operatives hurried into the Department of Geology, UNN and made their way to the HOD's office. Prof's secretary was taken aback by the unfolding scenario: the chief detective walked up to her and introduced himself. Without resistance, the Prof was arrested and whisked away in a black van while the other operatives carted away important files and documents.

The customs comptroller general of Nigeria trailed two cargo ships of unrefined crude oil en route to Abidjan and Lomé. Following a tip off by the Nigerian customs, the port authorities of the intended locations of the contraband were on red alert. Both ships were grounded, and their accomplices were apprehended on arrival. Interrogations were brief as the people on board were cooperative. Babayaro received a text a few hours later from an unknown number: *Your cargo has been confiscated, and your time is up!*

On reading the text, he pushed aside his lunch. Luckily, his family was away on vacation in the Netherlands, then he rushed to his bedroom, took some foreign currency, traveler's check, and his ECOWAS passport before heading out by road to the Kano International Airport to board a flight to the Netherlands. He disguised as an old man walking with a cane with a gray facial beard to evade security agents, which he did successfully before he met his waterloo. Onlookers were bewildered to see Babayaro hurried off in handcuffs.

The Prof and Babayaro were both placed in an undisclosed location. Days later, they were brought before the ad hoc committee on petroleum affairs for questioning before being charged to court.

Boma began work in earnest, setting up a think tank group to draw up a plan for the new agency. He developed a facility that grew *Nsukkadrilus mbae* specifically for the restoration of the Niger Delta cleanup process and introduced the project as WORMS OF BLACK GOLD CREEK. He outlined the recommendations of his findings and that of the senate ad hoc committee and developed a strategy to implement the clean-up processes of Ogoniland over a twenty-five to thirty-year period.

A day after hearing the news that he would be a proud father, he was brought to his knees when Tega called to tell him that Isabella had been kidnapped!

End

SUGAR LIPS

He who finds a wife finds a good thing, and obtains favor from the Lord.

—Proverbs 18:22 (NKJV)

October 2008

At twenty-eight, Tolu Badmus was already an accomplished business analyst, but at thirty-five, she fit the mold of the quintessential wife. She sincerely hoped that Zelda Pwadok's case would be on the favorable side of statistics. Tolu's cynicism was not unfounded. Bitter experiences were by and large her life's compass. Being married to Jide felt like living in a war zone. Insults exchanged hands like merchants while bloodied lips looked less severe to the feeling of senseless blackouts.

Tolu blamed everything on Ikenna's father. It was his father Comrade Amanze's diatribe against the government's dereliction of duty to the masses that caused his family to flee the country in 1993 on political exile. What difference did his eloquent speeches make? Is the country better of anyway? *Perhaps if Comrade kept silent, the gods wouldn't have dealt harshly with us.* Ikenna's departure was sudden, even to the delight of Mrs. Badmus who felt he lived a sheltered and protected life—a stark contrast to the erstwhile, prototypical rags to riches son-in-law, Jide. She could relate to Jide's life stories, but at whose cost?

On this day, the mass hysteria and compulsion of social media meant that failure to "like" Zelda's hint at an engagement would be perceived as bad blood. The possibility of one's blushes being spared on social media was unlikely. Reputations are smeared, families torn apart, fragile hearts shattered, and empires crumble with just a click of the button. Mrs. Badmus, Tolu's mother, liked it for the glitterati and could comb through social media for hours—often beating Tolu to the latest news. Both mother and daughter had something to talk about besides business processes and legal jurisprudence, but Tolu was taken unawares by what she was about to hear.

Tolu walked in to the living room to see her mom peering at the TV screen with her hands crossed across her bosom and her black-framed glasses sat comfortably across her nose bridge. Tolu always wondered why she never moved it up higher, after all it is called eye glasses, but it was of little importance at this time.

"How old are you now?" Mrs. Badmus asked.

Tolu was not sure why she was asking the rather obvious question. "Thirty-five, Mom," she answered.

"How old do you think I am?" Mrs. Badmus asked.

"Sixty," a bemused Tolu replied.

"I'm glad your math is good this time," Mrs. Badmus said, turning toward Tolu. "Which means at your current age, I was a mother of a ten-year-old," she concluded.

Mrs. Badmus reached for her phone on the coffee table next to her. All sorts of thoughts raced through Tolu's mind: *Don't tell me Jide leaked my bedroom pictures online. I am finished! I might as well kiss goodbye to potential husbands. May it never be well with you, Jide!* Mrs. Badmus handed her phone to a petrified Tolu.

"What do you see?" Mrs. Badmus asked.

"I see nothing," she replied. "Why did you make a big deal of this?" she asked.

"Well, obviously what you do these days is to 'like' every bridal picture like it's your newfound hobby." Then she asked, "When will you give me a grandchild?"

Tolu rolled her eyes back, feeling visibly irritated.

"I know you didn't just do that when your mother is still speaking," a crossed Mrs. Badmus said.

"But, Mom, you of all people know I am a victim of circumstance!" Tolu yelled.

"Watch your tone, young woman, I am still your mother," Mrs. Badmus reiterated. "You may now leave!"

Mr. Badmus, a professor emeritus of physics and astronomy at the University of Lagos, was the peacemaker when the two were at it, but he was away on a one-week-long official assignment. Tolu had every reason to blame her mother for her poor choice. For Mrs. Badmus, however, her daughter's allegations against Jide did not constitute prima facie—after all, she okayed him against Tolu's wishes.

After that long drive past the bridge to clear her head, ramshackle homes that dotted all over the lagoon like floating devices caused her to reflect.

Dad saw this coming all along; he could sniff out a person's personality from a mile away. Yes, he was right about Jide being a brute; but Mom talked him out of his fears, labeling his demeanor as the ultimate swag. I knew pain like never before. I cramped, I squealed, I cried my heart out when our unborn child couldn't handle the torture. It exited my body like a clump of blood. To think she would hit me below the belt is despicable! If only I listened to Dad about his reservations for Jide, I wouldn't even be giving Mom this pleasure of getting under my skin.

Tolu stormed into the house with one thing on her mind: leave her parents' house for good. Mrs. Badmus abhorred the phrase "I'm sorry"; perhaps it was antithetical to her posture as a magistrate.

Forcefully, she pulled her clothing from the hangers with reckless abandon. The wooden bar across the closet gave way, exposing a red, heart-shaped cardboard box which she had stowed away in her room since the nineties. A racing heart gave way to tremors as she reached for the box and set it on her bed. Her lips and hands trembled, and her throat felt heavy as sniffles gave way to warm streams of tears that bathe her eyes. Teardrops pelted the letters, pictures, and mementos that captured memories she and Ikenna shared at Zenith Academy.

*****

Zelda's apartment

Tolu arrived at Zelda's apartment later that evening to cool off for at least a week before deciding to return home or find a new place. Since Zenith Academy, Tolu and Zelda had been long-distant friends until now. Born into an oil-rich family, Zelda never knew struggle—everything in life came to her à la carte. Her tastily furnished apartment gave Tolu a temporary escape from the realities of a seemingly complicated life. Nightlife was not Tolu's forte, but Zelda was good company even if it meant tagging along.

"So, tell me, Tolu, when last did you do anything fun since your breakup with Jide?" Zelda asked.

"I've lost track of time to be honest, but if my memory helps at all…I can't even remember, that's how long it's been," Tolu replied.

"Are you kidding me?" a surprised Zelda asked. "But it's been over a year since your separation."

"The times at Zenith Academy in retrospect seem to be the best I ever enjoyed."

Zelda rolled her eyes. "And what about those times?" she loathed.

"Ikenna and I spent quality time visiting each other every week. We seldom loved the outdoors, but when we did go on picnic dates, we looked into each other's eyes with purity. He respected me as a lady. Just being around him was my high, a feeling of utter bliss!"

"You call looking at each other's eyes 'utter bliss'?" a sarcastic Zelda asked. "A relationship without the goodies is boring."

A curious Tolu asked, "So you mean love like this doesn't exist?"

Ikenna assured Tolu that he will not forget her, and she believed it most times. Soon after, Zelda's phone began to vibrate on the table. Both ladies were distracted by the noise and looked at the screen— the caller ID read "Lover Boy," but she declined the call. Again the phone vibrated and still it was "Lover Boy."

"I think you should answer the call 'coz he must truly be missing you." Tolu laughed.

"Naaah, he'll be fine. He is just too needy, and I can't stand guys like that." Zelda sighed.

"Before the calls, you were about saying something, right?" Tolu asked.

"Yes! Since he didn't come out clearly to make it official, then get over him," Zelda said with a smirk.

Tolu's little flame of hope was doused by Zelda's insipid response. Just as they had moved on to other topics, Zelda's phone vibrated once more. Tolu could not make out the caller ID. All she knew was that her friend's tone changed. It must have been an elderly person because she genuflected unconsciously while on the call, maintaining the least eye contact, which she thought was somewhat odd.

Zelda requested for the bill and suggested they leave for home.

"Is anything the matter?" Tolu asked.

"No, not at all," a flustered-looking Zelda responded.

A few more glasses of red wine at the apartment came in handy; thankfully, it was the weekend. Zelda snoozed away while Tolu watched a few more series of *Jealous Lovers* on a crime channel. The series must have been inundating enough for her to reach for the remote control. As she reached for the TV remote, Zelda's phone screen lit up, following a text from Sidekick: *I can't stop thinking about you. I want to come over for some midnight loving. Please, say yes when you get this message. That body is calling me...*

"Zelda, I am off to bed," Tolu said as she shuffled to bed.

While in the room, a feeling came over her *as she thought of Ikenna*; it was surreal. Slowly, she summoned courage to open the heart-shaped box seated on the dresser and picked up a rouge-colored harmonica. "Play this tune for me, darling," she said, closing her eyes.

*****

A new government emerged in 2006, and an olive branch was extended to the Comrade and his family. Before the Amanzes returned from political exile, Comrade and his wife decided that Ikenna's two younger siblings must have enrolled into college in the States. Even if they did return, Comrade would return first to test the waters before his wife, then his children—if they so desired. Both Comrade and his wife arrived one year ago.

As a pharmacy graduate from the historical Howard University, Ikenna was not known to sit on the fence on matters relating to nation building, bad governance, and followership. Ikenna of old, as described by close associates, was reserved but spoke like a wise old owl, wily as a fox, and possessed the memory of an elephant. Nowadays, Ikenna was a good-looking, well-rounded, young man, full of poise and with a heart of gold. Despite his accomplishments, one thing was missing—a wife. Plans were underway for him to return from the US to seal the deal with his wife-to-be. The date for the wedding was set for the end of the year. From time to time, he spent hours pondering what could have been had he not lost touch with Tolu. Holding fast to his promises was like taking an oath. Unselfishly, he missed out on potential relationships because he was bound by his words. Disappointing Tolu was never an option, but Imelda prevailed upon him to move on with his life when she learned of the marriage between Tolu and Jide.

Imelda was the link between Ikenna and Tolu in the early years of Zenith Academy. At twelve years old, her exuberant persona was endearing—always eager to please. Very quick in speed and speech, she frequently rescued Tolu from her parents' clutches during intense inquiries about Ikenna. Both lovers were fond of her. Imelda's sense of humor left one in stitches, and she often teased and toyed with the idea of falling head of over heels for a rich, romantic village tycoon.

Four years after Ikenna's sudden departure, Imelda went to college. Mrs. Badmus moved up the ladder to become a judge at the magistrate court, which caused the family to relocate to Lagos Island from the mainland. Visiting Tolu meant sitting in traffic for hours—it was a price too big for her to pay. Communication waxed and waned between Tolu and Imelda before fizzling off due to the demands of college, but somehow, Imelda was able to stay in touch with Ikenna. She was like a family member to Ikenna.

*****

At the mall

Life happened, and Tolu changed quite a bit: fuller lips, a voluptuous shape, and her every stride was as graceful as a swan. Imelda walked passed a lady at the entrance of the Mainland Mall; both glanced at each other for a minute. Imelda stopped to ponder who she reminded her of. Curiously, she followed behind her from a distance until the lady stopped to try out different shades of lipsticks. A feeling from within spoke about this lady's stride: it was "Tolu-esque." Searching for a beauty mole on the lady's right cheekbone would be a costly gamble for Imelda. So she pretended to check out the same brand of lipsticks.

"That's an expensive brand," Imelda said.

The lady glanced at her briefly and said, "It all depends on your preference."

"I mean it's the same effect that all brands aim to achieve, isn't it?" asked Imelda.

"You can look at it that way too," the lady replied.

Imelda kept up the conversation. "May I look at the colored lipstick you picked?" she asked.

As soon as the lady turned, she looked at the right cheekbone of the lady—there it was!

"Oh my goodness!" an excited Imelda yelled.

Tolu was in shock and wondered what kind of crazy fellow she was talking to.

"Tolu, you have changed quite a lot!" a surprised Imelda said.

"I beg your pardon, who are you?" Tolu asked.

"Who ran your risky errands for you and Ikenna?" Imelda asked, folding her arms.

Tolu's eyes got wide, and the bag she carried dropped to the ground. "Imelda!" she screamed.

The two were locked in profound embrace, and Tolu could not hold back her mascara-laden tears. Imelda was the last person Tolu envisaged to see. She apologized for her abrasiveness and offered to buy her the lipsticks of her choice. After all the social media buzz about Tolu's wedding, Imelda was shocked to hear gut-wrenching stories of her failed marriage. Tolu made two things clear in their discussion: that to ignore early warning signs—and think praying it away solves it—was the worst decision to make in life; on breakups and failed marriages, more emphasis are placed on the fanfare surrounding the wedding without focusing on the main thing, the marriage. Imelda discovered Tolu's finalized divorce papers were pending and encouraged her to believe in uncommon possibilities to find true love again.

Tolu did not hear her phone ring until the voice mail notification beeped: it was her dad

"I should be home now, Dad just called me," Tolu said.

"Can we meet Thursday, and may I have your number, please?" Imelda requested.

Later that night, Tolu returned home to see Zelda trying out a few outfits, mostly traditional evening wears—a signature specialty of Purple Label designers. The red, figure-hugging bedazzled lace gown sparkled with the slightest motion. Zelda's complexion shone vibrantly like the sun, courtesy of the off-shoulders and above-the-knee slit that exposed the side of her thighs.

Zelda tried a few more outfits, but Tolu stuck to the red one.

Tolu asked, "What's the occasion?"

"My dad's birthday is on Thursday, and from there, I am off for a cousin's wedding in Jos," Zelda replied.

"Lucky you…oh guess who I bumped into?" Tolu asked.

Zelda truncated Tolu's follow-up question. "No clue! And I'm not good at guessing either."

"Imelda!" Tolu exclaimed.

"Did she say anything about me?" Zelda inquired.

"Nothing, I volunteered the fact you've been kind to me to cool off at your place."

*****

Comrade Amanze had big plans for his son's wedding engagement and *iku aka*—typically a formal occasion by the Igbos to make known to the bride's family the intentions of the bridegroom.

Comrade's retinue boasts the likes of political stalwarts, business tycoons, oil magnates, and government officials. In fact, the vice president was rumored to be one of the expected distinguished guests.

As part of the preparations, Comrade was in Jos with his kinsmen to deliberate on the bride price and the litany of items on the bride's family list. Surprisingly, Comrade was taken aback when he learned that the bride-to-be's father—a gentleman extraordinaire—demanded less than a thousand Naira. This payment was to fulfil all righteousness.

Among other things, Comrade was a proud Igbo man, and he was caught in a dilemma of exposing his son to western values—with the hope that Ikenna kept his cultural roots. To complicate matters, his first son was to marry a woman of dual identities: a part from the north and another from the south. Left to Comrade, he would have wished for a lady of Igbo stock with homegrown values. The political upheaval in the country in the sixties—up to the turn of the seventies—fractured the country's polity along ethnic lines, causing deep-rooted mistrust. On the contrary, Comrade's love for "One Nigeria" resonated in his approach to dialogue and respect for his host's cultural nuances.

Comrade was one to plan ahead of time. So he called Ikenna on numerous occasions to confirm his arrival from Lagos to Jos. The stakes were high, and Ikenna could not afford to disappoint his father, let alone his mother who had distributed a bale of *aso ebi* (traditional uniform dress) to a plethora of her friends for solidarity.

*****

Tuesday's meditation

Imelda had just finished her morning devotions, and she pondered over, "For surely there is an end, and thine expectation shall not be cut off" (Proverbs 23:18). After talking to him, she paced about the room, asking herself if Ikenna was making the right choice for a wife. Most times, she felt Ikenna was too hard on himself. Thirty-nine was not a bad time to start a family; she made reference the story of Father Abraham conceiving Isaac when he was about ninety years.

Although Ikenna spoke glowingly of Tolu in the past, one thing was for sure, Ikenna will not compromise his principles when he takes the marriage vows. Disturbingly, Imelda's thought of Ikenna's words from their last conversation: *I have learned to take my chances* were loaded with meaning.

"Oh well," she said, "Ikenna would explain better when he arrives Nigeria."

*****

Marina Courthouse, Lagos

Judge Badmus (Mrs.) was on recess when she received the unsigned copy of the "Judgment of Absolute Divorce" between Tolu and Jide, which she unscrupulously retrieved from the Lagos High Court. The white parceled envelope read:

> CONFIDENTIAL
> C/o Hon. Judge T.A. Badmus
> Marina Courthouse, Tinubu Square St.
> Lagos, Nigeria

She put back the documents in the envelope and slipped it into her briefcase; thereafter, she scribbled a few lines on a writing pad. Hurriedly, she picked up her phone and sent for her official chauffeur. Having given the chauffeur firm instructions, she handed the sealed note to him and headed for the courtroom.

Approximately 5:00 p.m. that day, Mrs. Badmus received a call from Jide, acknowledging the receipt of the package and agreed to the contents therein.

"Who was that?" Mr. Badmus asked.

"Our son-in-law," Mrs. Badmus replied.

"That riffraff! What does he want?" a furious Mr. Badmus asked.

"Oh dear, can't the young man check on his in-laws again?" she spoke softly.

"As far as I am concerned, he is persona non grata in my house," Mr. Badmus insisted.

"You men and your egos, I just wonder," Mrs. Badmus said as she stood up from the couch.

*****

Wednesday to Remember

Zelda knocked at the door of the guest room while Tolu was fast asleep. "Tolu, I'm off to Abuja," she said, but there was no response. She left a handwritten note and money on the table for the cook to buy some food and fruits.

By noon, Zelda arrived at Abuja and was picked up by her father's chauffeur. Searching through her purse, she realized that the cake designer's card was missing. Tolu was now half awake when Zelda called.

"Zee, what's up?" Tolu asked.

"Hey, baby girl, sorry my trip was an emergency. I knocked at the door, but you were asleep," Zelda said.

Tolu sounded surprised. "Abuja, for real!" she asked.

"I know, but I'll tell you when I get back," she promised. "By the way, could you look up a number for me from a business card on my dresser?"

"Certainly!" she said as she headed for Zelda's room.

At the foot of the closet sat a pair of navy blue Salvatore Ferragamo men's loafers with a golden buckle. She picked it up to examine the shoes. It looked so similar to the one she bought for Jide on their first Valentine's Day as a couple three years ago. After all, anyone could have it, she must have thought.

*****

Ikenna arrived in Nigeria two days ahead of his sisters and headed straight for Eko Le Meridian Hotel where Imelda had made reservations for him. She arrived at the hotel at 4:00 p.m. and went straight to Ikenna's room. Ikenna opened the door to hear screams, followed with excitement; she jumped on him like a baby sister would do.

"Oh my! You are now a grown lady," Ikenna said, looking surprised.

"Gosh! You are such a hottie!" Imelda said, equally astonished.

Ikenna ushered her in and both sat down to catch up. Now he was ready to hear what surprise Imelda had in store for him. She spoke at length about a new chapter beginning where the last one stopped. Still, Ikenna could not comprehend.

Exhausted by her own rambling speech, she said, "I bumped into Tolu a few days ago."

Before she could complete her words, his grin widened—such was the effect Tolu had on Ikenna and vice versa.

"How soon can we meet her?" he asked.

"Can we take it slowly?" Imelda asked. "Tomorrow evening," she said with a cheeky smile.

*****

Thursday for Lovers

It was a busy day at work for Tolu, but the notification on her phone reminded her of the meeting with Imelda. From her office to the car and straight to the mall she drove. No time was left for makeup if she was to avoid the rush-hour traffic.

Before half past five that evening, Imelda and Ikenna were seated waiting for Tolu. Within thirty minutes, an elegant figure strutted through the lobby doors. Ikenna kept his cool as Imelda waved to get her attention; afterward, she walked toward Tolu to obstruct her view.

She motioned with her head and said, "Come, I have something to show you."

"Hello, love!" Ikenna said with a wide grin.

Tolu stumbled with a few steps and rushed to hug Ikenna like she never did. In his warm embrace, she began to weep profusely. Imelda looked away as she too began to well up with tears. Imelda signaled him then left to wait in their rented car at the parking lot.

"Why did you do this to me?" she said, hugging him so tightly.

Ikenna was speechless as black-dotted teardrops lined his white long-sleeve shirt.

"Why, why, why?" Tolu asked.

"It's okay, babe, cry no more," Ikenna begged.

Onlookers and shoppers alike thought it was a live movie set in action. Ikenna prodded her gently away from the direction of phone-happy recording bystanders. He never hid his distaste for the reckless use of social media. So the safest thing was to get her to the corner of the lobby.

"My life would have been better with you," she said, sniffling.

Ikenna dabbed her eyes with his handkerchief. "I never intended to leave for the States. You knew why we had to escape, didn't you?" he asked helplessly.

"Yes, my life too would've been better off," she concurred.

Imelda was scared because she saw the chemistry of old play out right before her eyes but happy that both could find closure. Fifteen minutes later, Ikenna and Tolu were sighted from the rearview mirror holding hands. Both came close to the driver's side of the rented car, and through the window, Imelda could see the passion in each other's eyes. While Ikenna attempted to wipe Tolu's tears, Imelda quickly inserted the key in the ignition and started the car—the sound jolted both of them apart.

"Babe, I'll see you tomorrow in the morning, right?" Ikenna asked.

"Don't you have to arrive a day before your traditional wedding?" a curious Imelda asked.

"My flight is for 7:00 p.m., so I'll be fine," he responded.

Both said goodbye, and he watched Tolu walked two cars away to hers. Clasping both hands over her head, Imelda feared the fire she stoked.

*****

After Tolu finished bathing that night, she played back each scene at the mall in her mind. One thought that slightly bothered her was Ikenna's wedding, but she shrugged it off smiling sheepishly. She picked up a pen and notepad by the bedside drawer and rekindled the poetic side of her—tapping from the numerous poems she wrote in her darkest times.

> My friend, my love, my Ikenna,
> You know me intensely…deeply…truly.
> The things you know I didn't tell you,
> You just know, and you know that you know.
> If I had known you like you knew me,
> Perhaps I would have seen it in your eyes.
> I would have heard your unspoken words,
> Utterances are sweet but those left unsaid are
>   even sweeter.
> I would have listened to the rhythm of your soul,
> I would have felt it in my heart that you loved me
>   like I did you.
> But then if you really knew me,
> You would have seen my doubts, my fears, my
>   insecurities,
> You would have told me you loved me with
>   assurance.
> A decade and a little more, you and I just found
>   expression,
> But to what end?
> Pray and tell…to what end?
> Can a love so true be lost?
> One so pure, so innocent.

*****

75

Sultry Friday

Daybreak could not come sooner for Ikenna. By 10:00 a.m., he was at Zelda's apartment where Tolu still camped out, leaving Imelda in the car. Her sweet fragrance of hyacinth and jasmine, the citrusy freshness laced with verbena, and the soothing woody fragrance of galbanum filled the living room. Ikenna could smell it through the door cracks. Inside the house, they locked in an embrace that felt like it was their last. Tolu's supple bosom pressed against Ikenna's chest; her warm, glossy magenta lips did all the talking. It wasn't part of the script, but Ikenna did not mind. Soon enough, he was reminded that he was only human as his heartbeat grew audible and his skin warm. His defenses surely were weakening for she was outright irresistible! Before the passionate kisses could intensify, he unlocked his lips and let out a sigh after letting her go of his tight embrace. Such was Ikenna's power of self-control.

The two held each other and waltzed to the sofa, looking into each other's eyes. Passionate stares became intense by the second, and intimacy was just a touch away. While seated in the car, the Bible verse of the day "What God has joined together, let no man put asunder" flashed before Imelda's phone screen. Three *ding-dongs!* startled both lovers. Tolu adjusted her top to secure her eye-popping cleavage.

Tolu looked through the peephole and grumbled, *Oh Lord, Imelda, you again?* She hissed like a snake and reluctantly opened the door.

"Hiii, Tolu! That's a gorgeous dress you've got on," a phony Imelda said.

"Thanks," Tolu replied turning back with a smirk.

"It's time to leave," Imelda beckoned Ikenna.

Ikenna tarried for a few more minutes talking about how well furnished Zelda's apartment was. Tolu recalled the day she felt Zelda had a crush on him at Zenith Academy, but she was the lucky one to win his attention because Ikenna considered her overly flirtatious.

Imelda became uneasy, and Ikenna excused himself to the bathroom. He stuck his head out from the corner leading to the bathroom. Tolu got the message and left Imelda whose back was turned away from Ikenna. Before long, Imelda realized what just happened and walked in the direction of the lip-smacking sounds emanating from the corner.

"We better be on our way to the airport to avoid the traffic," Imelda insisted.

When Ikenna stepped out, Imelda tugged Tolu to the corner and asked, "Are you out of your damn mind? For goodness sake, he will be married in December."

"Baby girl, 'all is fair in love and war,' so let me be," Tolu said with a smirk.

"Hmmm, this canoe you're rocking," Imelda said with a worried look.

Ikenna did not want to push his luck too far, so he gave Tolu one more hug and looked at Imelda, but she declined to give them another opportunity for sloppy kisses. No sooner than Ikenna exit the door, Imelda turned back to tell Tolu. "You'll thank me. Not now, but in the future." Then she shut the door behind.

*****

The flight to Jos that evening was turbulence-free amid the dark clouds. Zuma Rock Hotel & Lodge was the destination of the black Range Rover Sports car with license plate number AMANZE 1. The concierges were on ground to transport his suitcases to the presidential suite where his father and the rest of the family awaited his arrival. Among other discussions held, the review of program protocols and security were topmost on the agenda. Tolu's sensual kisses held him spellbound—with his thoughts wandering on occasions—often to the chagrin of Comrade. As he folded his arms across his chest to focus on the meeting, he felt something in his breast pocket. How it got into his pocket was like a mystery, but his first guess was as good as anyone's.

*****

Tolu pondered on a lot of things all through the day. *Yes, I know Jide was selfish, insensitive, and abusive, but not one to sleep around. If ever I saw signs of that, I think I would find out. We never checked each other's phones, so how would I have known? Jide's Salvatore Ferragamo shoes look like the one at Zelda's, but it'll be too much of a coincidence since she never saw eye to eye with Jide at Zenith Academy? Ikenna never mentioned his bride's name each time I asked. Imelda must know who she is...*

At 4:00 p.m. that day, Tolu headed for the family house; she had not been there since her father's return. Tolu liked to analyze things with her dad for he was calm and nonjudgmental. So on her drive home, she called her dad to run by the thoughts that flashed through her mind. Mrs. Badmus's ears propped up as she cleared her husband's dish from the coffee table and headed for the kitchen. She reached for her phone and sent a text to Jide.

While Tolu sat in an hour-long traffic, her phone beeped to alert her of a recent text from Jide, which read: My sweetheart, my world never remained the same since you left. I admit I was a coward, and I accept every adjective you describe me with. I have since been to anger management and counseling. Babe, just give me one more chance to make it right...

She slammed her phone in her handbag and sighed. No less than an hour had Tolu arrived at her parents' house that the doorbell rang. Mrs. Badmus was the closest to the door, so she opened it to usher in their visitor. The visitor walked into to the living room, and Mr. Badmus lifted his head and saw the dark, buffed, and bald-headed nuisance of a man, Jide.

"Who let this scalawag into my house?" a furious Mr. Badmus asked.

"Honey, honey, please, calm down, let's hear what he wants to say."

Mr. Badmus reluctantly sat down and wore a mean look on his face.

"Mom, what's this all about? Did you know about this?" Tolu asked.

"Jide, go ahead and speak like a man," Mrs. Badmus said.

Jide began shedding tears and said, "Good evening, sir and madam, I was a fool to let your daughter go. I have left my old ways, and I am a new man. Mr. Badmus, I betrayed your trust, and I did despicable things to her. Tolu, my love, I promise in the presence of your parents to be the husband you deserve."

With a loud wail, he prostrated at the feet of Mr. Badmus and asked for his forgiveness. Mr. Badmus stood up and walked away. Jide walked on his knees to Tolu to plead his case. Mrs. Badmus was careful not to push her luck with Tolu, so she rubbed her palms with a pitiful face. Soon enough, the sniffles transitioned to teary eyes and then wailing.

Ikenna was now off-limits while she was at a crossroad. Judging from her estranged husband's emotions, she felt it was a positive development. Tolu picked him up from the floor, and like a fountain, tears streamed down their cheeks. Mrs. Badmus joined them in their embrace. The couple passed the night in Tolu's room, and for the first time in the last year or so, they slept on the same bed.

*****

Saturday's Welcome

It was the last weekend of the month. Comrade and Ikenna left early that morning to Abuja to receive his wife and daughters. The hilly road that cut through the plateaus stretched for a few miles, flanked on both sides of the road by peanut farms scattered across the tropical savanna. Movement of automobiles was temporarily restricted by nomads and their cattle as they crossed the highway.

At 5:00 p.m., the Amanze's arrived at the Pwadok's compound with a fleet of expensive cars like Lamborghini, Ferrari, and Bentley among others. Griots at the entrance of the compound absorbed themselves in rapid ostinatos, plucking their *kontigi* (single-stringed lute) rhythmically. The Pwadok family was already seated in the visitor's lounge awaiting the Amanze's. Zelda's parents and some members of the extended family certainly gave the Amanze's a heartfelt welcome. Excitement aside, the Amanze's made their intentions known and all, and sundry were in agreement.

*****

November 2008

By the fourth week, Jide's pretense wore thin. Tolu was on the receiving end of a blow to her right breast that missed the chest. The painkillers were not enough to keep her pain-free, so she drove to the hospital the next day. She left the hospital with mixed feelings. Upon entry, she was diagnosed with "fat necrosis of the right breast;" before departing, her pregnancy test was positive.

As a devout Catholic, she was pro-life. Tolu was faced with the dilemma of trying to get rid of the baby and, on the other hand, free herself from her legal contraption with a ruse. Either way, she would lose him. If she must be with him, something had to give; the question was what, when, or how? To the Church of the Assumption, Ikoyi, she went to the Blessed Sacrament on bended knees to begin her novena prayers, imploring the intercession of the Blessed Virgin Mary. One day after the other, fervent petitions were made about her situation, asking for a miracle to end the marriage amicably and be with the one her heart beats for.

Hyperemesis gravidarum (nausea and vomiting during pregnancy) reared its ugly head. Tolu dreaded the mornings, hoping for the burden of dehydration and the feeling of being faint to pass her by. Strangely, on this fateful Saturday morning, she received snippets of an ongoing text in error from Imelda: *Tolu was all that you desire in a woman, but holding on to a decade old love just complicated matters. Words on the street were that she's back with Jide...*

By the time Imelda realized the slipup, she tried frantically to call and apologize, but Tolu switched off her phone. Imelda, once touted as an emissary, later a heroine, was fast becoming the axiomatic villain.

Tolu was saddened by this text, and soon enough the retching became severe. Hunched over the toilet bowl, she hungered for air as her chest tightened. The bathroom around began to look like a revolving stage. Every crawl felt like the hardest, but she persevered to reach the orange one liter Lucozade bottle by her bedside. Trembling hands unscrewed the cap, and with a few gulps, the orange-flavored glucose-water solution emptied.

Imelda's text snatched the wind from Ikenna's sails, and for hours, the news pierced his gentle soul. Pacing between the living room and the kitchen, the soon-to-be bridegroom caught a downcast look. Whatever the case, he believed Tolu would be honest with him. Ikenna picked up his phone and dialed Tolu's number. Now supine on the bed, Tolu heard her phone buzz: it was Ikenna. Her initial reaction was to decline the call, but on another note, she answered.

"Hello, Ikenna."

"Tolu, please, tell me that what I'm about to hear is false," he said.

After a slight pause, she said, "You heard right, and I am pregnant."

"Pregnant?" Ikenna asked.

"I am ashamed of myself and the poor choices I've made. I don't deserve you…" Tolu lamented.

"See, look, Tolu, I am not trying to—" Ikenna was interrupted.

"Of all people, you deserve someone better. Many waters have passed under the bridge. Please, move on with your life!" Then Tolu hung up and switched off her phone.

Jide was out binge-drinking with his friends that night while Tolu cried herself to sleep. In the early hours of Sunday morning, the ninth day of Tolu's novena prayers, Jide began to break out in cold sweat. He tossed about in his sleep and slipped into a trance, and the Virgin Mother in all her splendor illuminated his dark soul, and a voice said, "For every pain and sorrow you have caused my daughter, yours shall be double. And for the life of the innocent souls you have taken from her, their blood shall haunt you in the land of the living."

Jide tried to plead his case in the dream, but his lips were sealed, causing him to kick violently. The howl shook Tolu, who rose from slumber petrified. "What's the matter, Jide?" she asked.

Suddenly, she began to feel cramps, clutching the sheets, and within a minute, the sheets turned bloody. A frightened Jide looked at his wife and sprang from the bed to his feet and yelled, "Our marriage is over! I beg of you, leave and never return!"

Tolu was still getting to grips with the unfolding events when Jide grabbed his car keys and bolted through the doors. Soon after the contraction stopped, an inexplicable feeling of warmth and peace overwhelmed her—it felt celestial! She turned on her phone to call her dad, and the novena prayer reminder popped on the screen. Upon lifting her eyes to the ceiling, she returned the praise, "Blessed be God forever!"

Before the crack of dawn, Tolu was all packed and ready to go. She pulled her suitcases out of the door, stopped, and shook the dirt off her flat shoes before departing for good.

Jide made two frantic calls: first to Mrs. Badmus to tell her that he wanted out of the deal; second to Zelda, but she was unavailable. Mr. Badmus was curious about the early morning call his wife received, but she dismissed it as a customer service courtesy call. He was unsatisfied with the response, but her saving grace was Tolu's call. Mr. Badmus had the gut feeling that something was amiss.

"Tolu, is anything the matter?" he asked.

Quickly, he rolled out of the bed in his pajamas straight to the front entrance, and his wife followed. A fatherly embrace was all Tolu needed at this time. Her situation seemed to look like a game of chess played at the table of the gods.

*****

December 2008

It had been a little over a month since Imelda sent that accidental text to Tolu. Final year was no walk in the park, and so she needed to stay out of private matters—especially those that pertain to love. The first week of the festive season was relatively chill when her phone rang. When she flipped the phone, the caller ID was unknown. Somehow, she felt nervous but at the same time curious.

"Hello, Imelda speaking," she greeted.

An angry voice responded, "This is Tolu, don't you even think of hanging up."

"I messed up, Tolu. Please, forgive me, I am truly sorry," she pleaded.

"If you must redeem yourself, the time is now…" she said with all seriousness. "Who is Ikenna getting married to?" she asked.

Imelda paused for a few seconds to calm her nerves, but Tolu was not having any of it.

"Speak or I'll make you speak," Tolu threatened.

"Zelda!" Imelda said, quivering.

Before Imelda could say more, Tolu ended the call. Feeling betrayed on all fronts, she set out for Zelda's apartment. Luckily, the spare keys to the apartment came in handy. She barged into Zelda's room and snatched the business card for the cake designer and attempted to leave. Tolu's eyes locked in on the shoes once again, but at the spur of the moment, picked it up and headed for her car.

On the drive back, she recalled the conversation with Zelda about being boring in bed with Jide. Halfway through the drive on the third mainland bridge, those thoughts fueled her anger more; she picked up the blue shoes and flung it out the window in to the lagoon.

*****

By the second week, Jide had camped at his friends', switching between apartments to avoid being a burden. He was not only a nervous wreck, but his sex drive had shot through the roof and his desire for Zelda increased by the minute. His frequent calls were becoming increasingly irritating to the bride-to-be who was deep into her wedding preparations. Perhaps Jide was in denial that he was just a sport and, after all, Zelda's sidekick.

On this particular night, Jide could not sleep in peace when he returned to his apartment. The cries of wailing infants and Tolu's plea for mercy in his dream were harrowing. He was very troubled and irritable. So he placed a call to Mrs. Badmus, and as soon as she picked the call, she said "Don't you call me again!" and she hung up.

Jide was livid and thought out a plan while browsing through social media updates for Zelda's wedding. The next day, he withdrew some money from a depleting reserve set aside for emergency. Afterward, he set out with a bag to an unknown destination and left without it.

*****

Tolu's flight was scheduled to depart Lagos at noon for Jos tomorrow. She held all her cards to her chest, hoping to pull a surprise, or worst case, disrupt the wedding. All along, she only confided in her father but failed to tell him the purpose of her trip to Jos. Tolu reminisced the brief moments of bliss she felt while Ikenna was in Lagos and felt it so strongly to be a foretaste of brighter days. *What could possibly be the reason to ignore the obvious chemistry and compatibility we share? After all, the pregnancy failed—I am brand-new,* she thought.

As early as 6:00 a.m., Tolu waxed lyrically with a pen on paper about her future with Ikenna, and by ten that morning, she headed for the airport. Approximately one hour, twenty minutes from take-off, Tolu landed in Jos. She was consumed by a flurry of emotions such that she failed to appreciate the scenic view all through the drive. Twenty-five minutes later, Tolu arrived at a hotel in close proximity to the Rayfield Golf Course and retreated for the night. Something must give if she were to win Ikenna's heart again, and she was prepared to go the whole nine yards.

*****

Marina Courthouse, Lagos

Three men dressed in court robes and wigs alighted from a black Mercedes G-Wagon with briefcases. The court clerk was on hand to show them the office of Hon. Judge T.A. Badmus.

"Come in!" Judge Badmus said.

"These men here would like to see you, your honor," the clerk said, exiting.

"Thank you, clerk! Have a seat." She gestured. "What can I do for you, gentlemen?" she asked.

One of the men spoke. "We are here to get the 'Judgment of Absolute Divorce' which you seized."

"I beg your pardon!" she said, feeling insulted.

Simultaneously, they drew their pistols and pointed it toward the judge while the lead man swung around the table and put the muzzle to the side of her head. Mr. Badmus called his wife to tell her that Ikenna's wedding ceremony was on the pages of most dailies, but she could not answer. The man with the pistol to the head asked her to pick the phone up to return the call. Judge Badmus's hands trembled to a point of losing coordination.

"Do as I say," one of the voices said, "you will tell him to meet you at the Bar Beach, Victoria Island, by sundown." She did as she was instructed, but it left Mr. Badmus worse off.

"The documents?" They demanded one more time.

Slowly, Judge Badmus opened her briefcase with the confidential envelope.

"Sign it!" the lead man requested. "Now get up! You'll follow us to the car. If you move or attempt to cause a stare, we would not hesitate to pull the trigger," the leader threatened.

Judge Badmus obeyed every instruction till they got to the car and sped off.

*****

At the wedding

Preparations were underway, and the special guests were beginning to arrive. The vice president was the last to arrive with his convoy in the company of his security details. Blue and white balloons adorned the canopies and stands around the resort. White chairs lined the edges of the five hundred yards-long red carpets—fanning out from the center like a compass in six cardinal directions. Sounds of talking drums at the entrance and the highlife melodies ushered in dignitaries. The air smelled of expensive colognes and fragrances strong enough to numb olfactory lobes.

A call to rise from sitting position meant that the vice president had arrived, and the show only just began. The police band beat their drums, their horns blared and their cymbals clanked with pomp and pageantry—earning them a resounding applause after the national anthem.

The officiating clergyman was about to begin the exchange of vows when Tolu arrived the venue to take her seat behind the Amanze's entourage. Paparazzi jostled for every space to catch that picture-perfect photograph when suddenly three broad-shouldered men who posed as cameramen pulled out semiautomatic guns from their camera bags and opened fire in the direction of the soon-to-be wed couples.

Stunned by the commotion, the couples dispersed in the direction of their families—Tolu followed in the Amanze's direction. Swiftly, the secret service scurried the vice president and other dignitaries to safety while police details and military escorts responded bullet-for-bullet with unrivaled ferocity!

Had the assailants known of the status of dignitaries in attendance, they would have reconsidered launching such a brazen attack. Ten minutes of rapid fire seized, leaving the assailants severely wounded. First aid treatments were given to preserve their lives. From the scene to the ambulance, investigations had begun. Citizens nationwide were glued to their TV screen as preliminary investigations linked one "Jide Pedro" as the brain behind it. A manhunt for Jide was launched!

Mr. Badmus was petrified and called the police on his way to the designated pickup location. He arrived at the beach just when the police located Judge Badmus who was bound facedown. As soon as the judge saw her husband, she hugged him like a child crying, telling him what a foolish wife and mother she had been. Mr. Badmus was more thankful that she was alive than care about her apologies.

*****

A week after the incident at the botched marriage ceremony, Zelda's father's oil exploration license was revoked by the federal government. Consequently, Zelda was disowned and stripped off any family inheritance. Rumor had it that she left the shores of the country pregnant for her sidekick.

Mr. Badmus feared the worst when he handed his wife a letter from the Nigerian Bar Association. Her head dropped in shame: she was suspended as a judge pending further investigations linking her with Jide.

"What is it, darling?" her husband asked. She handed him the letter, and the look on his face was one of disappointment.

*****

Comrade and his family loved Tolu as theirs. Since graduating from pharmacy school, Ikenna had never been this happy. What impressed the Amanzes was Tolu's beauty, brawns, grace, and warmth—she worked tirelessly on the interior decorations at the family's newly built stately mansion by Lake Oguta. The pleasant aroma of freshly cooked vegetable soup, the roasted yam and spiced palm oil sauce, and the ecstasy of the villagers when the *mmanwu* (masquerades) performs at the market square made Tolu imagine how fulfilled life would be as *Obi di ya* (the heart of her husband).

Ikenna was due to leave for the States the following day, and in her usual way, Tolu packed his suitcase. The plane ride from Owerri to Lagos was too short for Tolu, but every nautical mile was worth it. Tolu was the last to give Ikenna a farewell hug, but in his ears, she whispered, "*Obi m* (my heart), don't open this note until you're airborne!"

"I love you, baby," Ikenna said.

At thirty-two thousand feet above sea level, the accent was complete. Ikenna reached for the note in his breast pocket. Tolu's words read:

> Obi m, what's done is done. Now I know how it feels to lie in your arms and look into your eyes and taste your sugar lips, Walk hand in hand, and grow old together. Fifteen years later, this thing that we feel remains and stronger still. In becoming, we have found expression, arms is where I belong. Now I can feel your pulse…align to your rhythm. The world waits while we embrace, and when we kissed, sweet electricity rage the human body. That's what you do to me. I feel like a woman…your woman. We are at peace, and we are content. Now that you've put a ring on it, I am one with you, my love… This shall be to us a symbol of love, now and in the afterlife… Last night you told me that "Life imitates art, and art imitates life," so from my heart, this keepsake is just for you.
>
> *Surely there is a God, and He rules over the affairs of men.*

End

AFTER THE SIGN

Be not impatient in delay, but wait as one who understands...

—James Allen

It took Nnedi five years to conceive Chidubem after her marriage to Jacob. Tolerance had become a byword for this daughter-in-law. Endurance she had to have, or succumb to the tirades of Jacob's mom which happened ever so often. Grandchildren are every potential grandmother's dream; her mother-in-law needed them since Jacob was the only child. Nnedi took it in good fate, for she knew their testy relationship was born out of desperation and frustration. From one doctor to the other, medical advice—even as far as the US—became a price too costly to bear. Not deterred by her diagnosis of premature ovarian failure, Nnedi believed miracles still existed. Twenty-five years later, her pride and joy is all grown-up: a fine, brilliant, young man.

Jacob was her rock through barren times, in turn, her support for him was unwavering. Both had a united outlook, spoke with one voice, but the decision to let Chidubem (Dubem) study abroad was more than she could contend with.

"Darling, Dubem is too young to venture out into a foreign land far from us."

"Honey, how many times will I tell you he is no longer a boy?"

"All you men talk like that," she said, "we mothers know what we feel."

"What feeling? He is a young man for goodness sake."

"You wouldn't understand."

"I hope it's not that psychic prediction foolishness?"

"Death would knock on our son's door when he turns thirty! You call it foolishness, Jacob?"

"All fake stuff. They guess all the time!"

"I've never met her before, she stopped to tell me," she explained. "What if she's right?"

"Honey, sweetheart, I think you're having separation anxiety."

"Don't patronize me."

"Okay, honey, let's talk about this later. I'm running late for my appointment."

What Nnedi failed to tell Jacob was that the soothsayer spoke of the possibility of forestalling it. It didn't matter anyway, Jacob would still have laughed it off.

These days, Nnedi's pastime was tending to her beautiful rose garden—replanting, planting, and transplanting flowers to the soil. Since her retirement, she took to horticulture as a hobby, but she was amazed to see it became a business venture.

A month had passed at lightning speed; July arrived. In mid-July, their son was due to depart for Washington, DC, to begin college at the University of the District of Columbia. Dubem and his father loaded the truck, and everything was good to go.

"I wonder what's holding up Mom?" Dubem asked.

"Nnedi, we'll be late for the airport!" Jacob yelled.

She was completing her novena prayers where she handed over her son to the Blessed Mother to be his motherly guide.

"Ah-ah! I wonder what the rush is?" she asked. "After all, the airport is not so far."

Nnedi anticipated a long drive to the international airport. Could she have forgotten that Lagos, a city with incurable optimists, thrived both in chaos and order? It is a city where thrilling tales of gridlock maneuvers conferred one with "street credibility." Avoiding the bumper-to-bumper traffic in Lagos often defies logical permutations. In a matter of seconds, cases of road rage, motorists hurling insults at taxi drivers could bring the flow of traffic to a standstill; nonetheless, their drive was hassle-free. Whatever transpired along the drive was of little importance to father and son, both cracking a few jokes in between. At the passenger's corner sat Nnnedi, aloof to the realities of the moment. Jacob, on occasions, spoke words to steer away his wife's thoughts, but it did not work.

"Are you still brooding over that issue?" Jacob asked.

"What issue, Mom?" Dubem asked.

"It's nothing, son, Mom is just thinking of the backlog order of flowers."

"Common, Mom, the one person able to take care of it is you."

Nnedi glanced at Dubem and nodded in approval and smiled half-heartedly. Jacob gently squeezed her hand and held it for the last fifteen minutes of the drive.

Summer travels were unusually busy: both departure and arrivals witnessed a few delays. The journey was ten hours long, but the delays meant that 8:00 p.m. departure time was now 10:00 p.m. Six hours wait time was no joke, so Jacob, Nnedi, and Dubem kept busy—switching from serious talks to bursts of laughter. No one cared if they were loud: the airport was loud at this time anyway. The temperature inside the airport had ticket agents rigorously rubbing their palms together, some grabbing lightweight shawls while most passengers sat sideways with hands in between their legs. Travelers were not in this alone, even trolley wheels squealed in protest against the temperate hall.

"Announcing the arrival of Delta Air Line flight 658 from Atlanta. Passengers, please, proceed to Gate 24 for boarding…"

Probably the lady behind the voice was slender-framed, shapely, and maybe in her midthirties: a sure pick for any model agency. All of that didn't matter to Dubem whose personal emotions sought for his attention like two competing wives.

"Common, let's see you off to the security." Jacob chuckled. "The point of final goodbyes."

"Dubem, come and sit here and save your auntie and uncle's numbers on your phone," she asserted. "It's important so that you don't get stranded at the airport." She scrolled up and down the screen of her phone close to a minute, fiddling with the contact list.

"Nnedi, the young man needs to go through security," Jacob said. "Just text it to him so he'll receive it when he arrives."

"Honey, you're sounding a little impatient, and it's not helping matters."

"Mom, you're going through a long process—"

"Children of nowadays think technology left us behind."

"What's happening is already proof," Jacob said.

Dubem reached for her phone. "Let me help you out."

"And you think you know how to operate my phone. Ehn?" asked Nnedi.

A few taps and scrolls and it was done. Phone numbers went through in thirty seconds.

"Okay, Mom, let's go."

"Oh wait, did you check to see if you forgot the ground prawns I left on your reading table?"

"My goodness," Jacob said, growing a bit impatient. "Well I'm sure you can purchase the next flight ticket if he misses it."

Nnedi barely moved Dubem's clothes inside the suitcase. "Oh, it's here."

"Are you done now?" Jacob asked.

"Emmm I think—"

Jacob didn't want further delays, so he pushed the trolley; Nnedi followed behind and then Dubem. Nnedi toyed with the idea of offering to pay the difference to move the flight by one week. Her brisk pace notwithstanding, the numbers strung together in her head, bounced back and forth.

One last hug from Jacob and finally the moment of truth beckoned. A flurry of emotions seemed to descend on Nnedi like dark clouds; the feelings of a lump too big to swallow and that of breathlessness were surreal experiences.

The words "Don't cry, Mommy, everything will be fine" could not console her. Jacob's feet stayed glued to the ground, helpless and wished Nnedi could just hold the sniffles till they got to the car.

"It's okay, my love, Christmas is just a few months away." Jacob had a way of convincing Nnedi to believe anything. If his incorrigible optimism watered her garden, which sprouted Dubem, who was she to think otherwise?

As Dubem felt her embrace weakening, his lips quivered a "Goodbye, Mom." From mother to son, an eternal bond transmuted from the physical to the spiritual. Tomorrow was unknown, but through the maternal bond, she would feel Dubem's pulse from a distant land.

*****

Olivia, an only child of Betty and Marco Nunéz, was five when they immigrated to the US from the Philippines. Her happy childhood was a distant haze as the realities of a new world dealt the Nunéz's a fair share of hopelessness. But at their lowest moments, Marco held on to the masterfully penned poem which she (Olivia) recited for inspiration on numerous occasions: "Give me your tired, your poor, your huddled masses yearning to breathe free, the wretched refuse of your teeming shore. Send these, the homeless, tempest-tossed to me. I lift my lamp beside the golden door."

Olivia saw faith at work firsthand. If they could get past those bitter days, she thought, climbing Mount Everest was a cheap feat. She adored her father and was inseparable from her mother. Of all things she loved her father for, she hated one thing: the charred cigarette butts heaped on crystal ashtrays. To recall such habits would not be complete without mentioning the day her dad slumped on the couch with a cigarette in his hands. Smoke detectors howled recklessly—all competing for the one that squealed the most. Huge bursts of white smokes puffed across the door frame as she raced down the stairs. Garlic-like smell of arsine stifled the little oxygen left in the room. Olivia's father's sweet call of "Livy" was now stowed away in the recess of his soul, her world reduced to rubbles.

Life was all about choices. She learned that individual actions, whether good or bad, affect others—failure to realize this sums up escapism. Betty's prolonged weakness and maroon-stained handkerchiefs—a consequence of secondhand smoking—was enough to make Olivia a staunch advocate for tobacco ban. Today's tobacco lobbyist would swarm and sting Olivia like killer bees if she went on a prohibition campaign.

Weekend pleasures were restricted to a few flashbacks of Olivia's routine. Early morning jogs with Munchkeen (a Jack Russell Terrier), cooling off with vanilla coffee latte with bites of chocolate-filled éclair, followed by Zumba sessions before noon cost her a few pounds. Her mom's survival was worth more than her priced hourglass figure, which had no rival at Providence Hospital, Washington, DC, where she worked as a nurse. Nowadays, Room no. 307 at the Med/Obs floor was a temporal home. Betty's final days were memorable because of her compassionate daughter. On some days, Olivia spent most of her weekends shuffling between home and hospital while she slept over at the hospital off duty days.

Last week would have been catastrophic for Olivia had her mother not been vigilant. It was her daughter's gasping snores that woke Betty up, but the short burst of muffled pleas underneath Olivia's breath piqued her interest. If only she knew Olivia was trapped in a hypnagogic state of mind, haunted by a knife-wielding butcher that held her mom captive. Betty panicked, reached for Olivia to prevent a fall. For a brief moment, Olivia was startled.

"Livy, you have to get your rest. You need to take care of yourself!"

"Mom, I am fine, you—"

"No, no! I feel stronger than I was. It's not worth losing two people…I mean two people don't have to be sick at a time."

"Don't say that, Mom, be positive."

"Positivity is overrated. By the way, Munchkeen needs you, he hasn't been fed, I suppose," she reminded Olivia. "Poor thing!"

"Mom, I would rather you take your meds and not rub it in."

Olivia stretched for the pill sorter by the corner of the bed and handed it to Betty. Then she felt for her purse, which fell on the floor; she picked it up and dusted it. One look at her mom and she said, "A dog forgives, but I can't live a life of regret knowing that life is fleeting." She left.

Betty welled up, tossing her magazine to the end of the room. Given the chance, she would have retracted her words, but it was ill-timed. It came from a place of love, but Olivia was headstrong yet selfless to a fault, and that scared Betty.

Lately, Olivia had gained a few more pounds; stress was written all over her face. On her next visit, as both agreed, Olivia was to leave if Betty slumbered. Betty pulled a few fast tricks, closing her eyes the moment she heard Olivia by the door. A week after the resolution, Betty started mumbling words, coming in and out of consciousness, unable to eat. Intravenous lines (IV), EKG leads crisscrossed her chest; green-webbed veins were visible beneath her skin.

On the eve of Thanksgiving, November 23, 2006, Betty's eyes flicked open, and she moaned, looking hapless. The movement of the IV lines alerted Olivia whose world was immersed in a telenovela.

"Mom!" Olivia said, looking surprised before leaning toward Betty.

"*Cough! Cough!* "I want you to bring my trinket box. Mama Rosa wants me to give you her wedding ring."

"What ring?" she asked.

Betty grimaced as she adjusted her posture to say, "My daughter, remember that 'we are blind because we choose not to see, we are deaf because we choose not to hear. We fail to see the future because we ignore the present.'"

"What do you mean, Mom?"

"It will all make sense after the sign."

Olivia's question was excusable as a nurse to ask, "Mom, what year is this?"

Betty glanced at the door. "Now hurry home and be back so we can watch the next episode of *Saints and Sinners*."

Relieved at her response, Olivia promised, "I'll bring your favorite soup on my way back." Olivia shut the door, then Betty's ocular muscle began to weaken as she recited "Agnus Dei." After a deep breath, the cardiac monitor flatlined.

While Betty's ghostly voice lingered on in Olivia's head, she tried to work out how much time it would take before returning to the hospital. She thought, *Thirty minutes, just enough time to feed Munchkeen and take a quick shower.* Munchkeen was a happy camper after some Pedigree treats—running from one end to the house to the other. As she opened Betty's closet to the right, she saw the trinket box. Munchkeen barged in, looking backward and barking. It moved sideways, spun left and right, paused then faced the curtain and continued to bark and bellow. Olivia turned to her dog and shushed it, but it continued. "What a strange boy you are," she said.

Both showering and getting dressed was the quickest ten minutes since nursing school. By the time she got to the hospital room, the nursing assistant was just about to remove the linen. Olivia's heart sank.

"Where the hell is my mom?" she asked.

Before she got a response, Janet, the shift supervisor, interrupted, "Olivia, may I have a word with you, please?"

"Can someone tell me what's going on?"

"I'm sorry to say," Janet said with remorse, "she didn't make it—Olivia! Olivia!"

From the opposite side of the hallway, Monae and Lucy, the on-call nurses, ran toward the scene to help Olivia from the floor.

"Lucy, get me an ammonia inhalant!" Monae said.

In a few seconds, Olivia's eyes opened, and she lost track of what happened. Monae was the strongest of the three, so she helped Olivia up.

"What are you guys doing here?" Olivia asked, and suddenly she realized what just happened. "Mom! Where is my mom?" she yelled.

"I'm sorry, she couldn't make it," Janet replied.

Tears streamed down Olivia's face before Janet uttered another word. Sniffles turned into inconsolable cries.

"Come, I'll walk you to the morgue," Janet said, extending her hand.

Janet held Olivia close to her side and thanked both nurses for their help.

"We hope you feel better," Lucy said, departing with Monae.

*****

Olivia's nights of sudden awakening and profuse sweating lasted for three months. Life started to feel normal. Throughout the grieving period, Munchkeen was her solace. Betty's lifeless body remained a haunting image—choosing moments to appear and reappear in Olivia's mind. To think that the soul finds rest in death and, on the contrary, feel their energy and appear to loved ones remains a mystery. Perhaps the transitory phase to the yonder realm is the last chance to instruct loved ones.

Christmas Eve was the strangest feeling for Olivia. Make-up shifts in the last month since her mother passed was crucial to meet her financial obligations. All she wanted to do this particular night was to get as much sleep for the next two days before resumption. In her dream, the women dancing in a banquet looked alike but distinct in the robes they donned. A turquoise-like ring exchanged hands before it was handed to her by the younger-looking female. Once the ring got into her hands, she shook violently into wakefulness. The feeling petrified her. Suddenly, she realized what the message was. In no time, she rushed to the closet and opened the trinket box then tossed the contents on her mother's bed. There it was, the ring! Just as she held up the ring to admire it, the box dropped and exposed a handwritten note. Courage was absent, but she cringed as she stooped to retrieve the paper. Olivia's jaw dropped! *It must have been a mistake,* she thought. Her mother lived a modest life, but to leave monies to clear her school debts and use the remainder for a noble cause was unheard of.

*****

The last two years of Dubem's college education was a salvage mission. He knew that the hard-earned currency—moved from one financial clearinghouse to the other—would have been a waste had he not turned the corner academically in his junior and senior years. Jacob and Nnedi were proud parents as they watched their son pick up a departmental prize. That year of graduation was agog with dignitaries from far and wide. Some families arrived with panache and aplomb to the admiration of students and visitors. A healthy Caribbean and African students' rivalry ensured that the top two graduating students from the school of engineering in the last two years were islanders. But this year, the ultimate prize went to the

African students. It felt as though the parents from the continent knew what was in the offing, they came prepared. Like a sea of corals, vibrant-looking *geles* (head ties) shone around every section of the room, obscuring the view of a disgruntled few. Thundering applauses and vociferous cheers from the African parents and families subdued others; indeed, they stole the show. In fact, so inspired was the master of ceremony that he spoke about tracing his ancestral roots to the Island of Bioko, Equatorial Guinea.

Since Dubem graduated, he was two years between jobs and disillusion. Just about the same time, Isoken, his girlfriend, was in his life. Dubem's obsession for being his own boss drove Isoken crazy few and far between, but most times, she loved his drive and resilience. Rigorous gym sessions were a let out for Dubem's job rejections, which by and large were a handful. All his college friends relocated after graduation, but DC felt like home away. These days, he could not fathom living with his girlfriend, let alone being catered to. A situation his ancestors would frown at. After all, times have changed. Back then they never knew much about their wives. *It's important nowadays,* he thought. So he considered the idea of moving in with Isoken.

By the fourth month, both lovers' fondness toward the other chipped away. Subtle jabs were labelled as jokes, but soon enough, it turned vile. Dishonorable talks like "Hey, young man," "shameless thing," replaced the allure of "Hey, sweetie" and "Sugar dumpling." On other days, Isoken could rouse an army with positive words of encouragement then flip moods to the other extreme. The relationship degenerated to a no-speaking spell, which lasted for more than a week.

On a fateful spring morning, Dubem received a call for an interview, which was slated a week from the notification. He kept the news of the interview to surprise Isoken, most likely for a tongue-in-cheek. Excited about the prospect of a new job, he called his mother.

"Mom, I have some good news for you," Dubem said with enthusiasm.

"Son, what news?" she asked.

"It's the recent job I applied for," he said, "I have an interview lined up with them."

"How much is the salary?" she asked.

Dubem was shocked to hear the question that followed. "When do you start?"

"How can I start when I haven't been interviewed?" he asked.

"I don't question your abilities and poise," she said, sounding confident. "Always keep God first despite the odds…I love you, son."

"Thank you, Mom," he said with a feeling of heaviness in his heart.

Meanwhile, Isoken turned in a thirty-day notice to leave the apartment and was out house hunting. Dubem was aloof to her plans and took her silence for granted. The day of the interview, he received a text from Isoken stating that their relationship was over. Dubem was fortunate not to check the text before his interview, which now was uncertain following his perceived poor performance. It felt like his world was finally over when he read the text. On a busy street, everything around him seemed static and unfamiliar, and in a blink, he spiraled five feet above the ground and landed on a parked car on the side of the street. Onlookers thought the worst! Within minutes of impact, people of all shades gathered around him—some making frantic distress calls.

*****

It seemed to be the season of irresponsible financial impunity for banks in the country. Clover Leaf Bank's financial bottom line was abysmal. Jacob was laid off three months ago, and this troubled him daily. The thought of being a dependent was a constant thorn in his flesh. To depend solely on Nnedi was an anathema. Nnedi was a woman of character, and had a mind of her own, but she knew when to draw her battle lines—those times seldom occurred because Jacob was so secured a man.

In recent times, however, Jacob became headstrong on purpose solely to clear any doubts that he was still the man of the house. The question was, for what reason and at whose cost? Never was it known that the world lost sleep for the weary; rather, it celebrates the attainment of fortune from the cruelties of misfortune.

Life never stood still for those who grumbled, but Nnedi had a mind to always look ahead. Commanding her day with eternal understanding, compared to Jacob's life of practicality, showed wisdom is never a function of being a figurehead—Nnedi's results were visible for the reckoning.

It was impractical to demand of Nnedi the kind of patience and willpower she exercised during the trying periods, but she proved innumerable chauvinists wrong. From the outside, it was impossible to tell who the breadwinner was for she sustained her family with utmost humility and grace. Jacob was overwhelmed with emotions, but he composed himself to express his feelings.

"I've all along been petrified of the day you'd ridicule me for not being the provider I once was," he said with a sniffle.

This was Nnedi's first time to see her husband emotional; she was quick to embrace him. "Love, you are my wealth, not what your bank account says," she said.

"But for how long, Nnedi, will I let you do this yourself?" he asked.

"Money maybe a source of satisfaction, but your love is my drive," she said, looking into his eyes.

Jacob had no words in his lips to utter.

Nnedi continued. "God has placed honor on you. I am not threatened to say so because in you, I've found the way to chase my dreams," she said, holding his hands. "Gibraltar is like a mountain too small to surmount when you've got me."

At the end of her affirmation, Jacob's ego departed far away from his consciousness.

Later that night, in a dream, Nnedi recalled the words of the soothsayer; she awakened and was drenched in sweat. Between reciting her prayers and trying to fall back asleep, the thought of Dubem caused her heart to race. For three hours, sleep fled her troubled mind. Restless, she roused Jacob up in a manner that irritated him. Before Jacob could question the disturbance, she shared the dream to him. The vivid dream—told twenty-five years ago—still felt like yesterday. As usual, he dismissed Nnedi's trepidations.

When the day broke, Nnedi placed a call through to Dubem, but it rang severally without a response. She texted and waited thirty minutes for a reply that never came. Frantic calls to Isoken proved futile. A troubling sensation overwhelmed her, and she felt woozy; luckily, Jacob was on hand to intervene.

A frustrated Jacob said, "Honey, you need to stop worrying for no reason."

"My only child is in trouble," she responded with a feeble voice.

"Now, please, don't tell me it's this imaginary soothsayer feeding you all these legends."

"Jacob, you still don't get it…"

"My oh my," he said, already exasperated, "just bury this topic, it's becoming annoying!" Jacob gave her a glass of water and left for his study room.

Isoken was not going to have another round of incessant phone calls from Nnedi, so she called Dubem, but it went straight to voice mail. "Young man, please pick up the damn phone 'coz your mom has been blowing up my damn phone!" she said.

*****

Dubem arrived at Providence Hospital in an ambulance amid a traffic logjam on Michigan Avenue, Washington, DC—straight to the ICU. Nothing but the beeping sounds of cardiac monitors and breathing machines echoed tunes of despair for Dubem's comatose body. Nurse Lucy checked her patient's IV lines and vital signs one last time before her shift was over. She pitied the helpless young man who lay motionless before her for the past five days.

By sundown, the bus schedules had slowed down, so it was better for him to attempt a thirty-minute walk home. At the corner of a junkyard, a ferocious pack of mean barking dogs surrounded a smaller dog—each attempting to lunge at every move. He hadn't seen a thing like this before. The smaller dog had something in its possession that the bigger dogs wanted, but it put up a resistance amid its piercing howls. For how much longer the smaller dog could put up a fight was unclear. His walking pace increased, then he stepped aside from the sidewalk to pick a branch blown off from a tree and dashed toward the scene.

One after another, he swiped at the pack of dogs, hitting and missing some. Like true packs, they dispersed at all corners to assess the threat; they regrouped and lunged in synchronizing fashion. Bolting toward him was a pit bull with a head the size of a fully grown pumpkin; it had to be the pack leader. He wasn't going to miss the hit or else he'd be a delicate piece of lamb chops for the entire pack. What was to come called for a steady hand and heart. He lost sight of the other distractions behind as he felt a lancinating pain from the fangs that dug into his right calf muscles that ran through his spine, which caused him to blink! As his eyes opened, the ferocious pack leader in a full display of aerodynamics was an arm's length from his windpipe. Bam! The wild swing splattered gooey saliva on his face as he knocked the pack leader to the ground. With their tails between their legs, the pack leader and the rest dispersed in a swift retreat.

While he tried to catch his breath before leaving the spot, the smaller dog barked to get his attention. Cautiously, he walked toward what looked like an injured dog. As he attempted to pick the dog up, the cell phone's screen came alight! Apparently, it was the object the bigger dogs attempted snatch from the smaller dog. He tapped on an icon that unveiled vital information pertaining to the health of the small dog for a brief second. Suddenly, the phone shut down!

"Hello, Mr. Dubem, I am Olivia, your nurse for the day," she said with enthusiasm, but he was still unresponsive. Olivia's week-long break was cut short following a nursing shortage. On this day of resumption, she was floated between the ICU and Med/Obs unit. As she settled in to review his vitals, the IV lines began to move. Olivia was elated that Dubem was coming around! It was a thing of pride for her, perhaps judging from the fact this was his first time since his admission to respond to stimuli. He was in an unfamiliar territory, so he was disoriented and agitated, and the attending doctor stabilized him. Very early the following morning, he was transferred to the Med/Obs floor.

Nurse Monae, a six-foot-tall blond was assigned to Dubem on the Med/Obs floor for that day. Colleagues loved her company, and her vivacious nature was infectious—often with a glistening white smile. Instantly, she made an impression on Dubem. It was evident to the other nurses that Dubem was fondly attached to Monae. On days when she was on duty, Dubem malingered the most, feigning frequent headaches every four hours just to get Monae's attention, and it enabled him to get his temples massaged. Sadly, he was a difficult and petulant patient toward Lucy, and most especially, Olivia. The latter two had come to terms with the fact that he had a special attachment toward Monae.

Lucy discovered the handoff notes by the paramedics as she was charting her notes for the day. Isoken's phone number was listed as an emergency contact. Then she remembered that the last time a call was made to the contact on behalf of Dubem, a female's voice was heard on the answering machine. She hoped that it would be Dubem's girlfriend. Perhaps she was fed up with the petty jealousy that swirled inside her. Surprisingly, Monae was the least voluptuous compared to Lucy and Olivia, but she wasn't far from having their kind of physique.

Isoken was notified about Dubem's accident; she arrived at the hospital that evening and headed toward Dubem's room on the third floor. At first, she had a cautious approach toward his room amid the sounds of laughter. She cracked the door open and stared at the blond-haired lady in the room.

"And who are you, precisely?" Isoken asked.

"Pardon me, ma'am, I'm Duby's nurse for the day," Monae responded.

Isoken had a surprised look on her face. "Oh, Dubem, this nurse now call's you, 'Duby,' eh?" she asked.

"What difference does it make?" he asked. "After all, you've moved on," Dubem said, frowning.

Monae was a little confused but tried to calm frayed nerves, but Isoken was not having any of it.

"Hey, look here, nurse, don't you have patients to look after, or whatever?" she asked.

"Patients like this gentleman here," Monae replied.

Isoken snapped back at her. "I beg your pardon!"

"I'm just doing my job, ma'am," she said with a wry smile.

"You know what, smart-ass," she said, "please, leave this room!"

"Actually, I was about to before you came in," Monae replied.

Perhaps Monae got a kick out of Isoken's frustration, flipping her hair sideways as she walked past Dubem's unfriendly guest.

"Please, shut the door behind you," she requested. "Such brazen disrespect coming from a nurse."

Dubem was already fed up with the mini spectacle that ensued and was not about to start another.

"Isoken, I have done nothing to deserve this embarrassment from you," he said. "Have you come to steal what's left of my happiness?"

"Babe, please, relax, this is not the time to get worked up," she answered.

*****

For Monae, opening up to her colleagues at the nursing station was never a good idea. Lucy and Olivia laughed their lungs out—even more so with the confused look on their friend's face.

Dubem returned to the operating room for wound dehiscence repair along the incision on his right hip. After work hours, Isoken visited Dubem at the hospital three days in a row. She often treated him to rice, beef stew, and plantain, his favorite dish. The aroma was so tantalizing that it had the staff salivating even after their lunch breaks. Others aside, Isoken's sudden care was puzzling to Dubem.

Each time Dubem's pain medication was administered late, he got edgy and slightly delirious—lashing out at minor instances.

Lucy got her fair share of Isoken's shades almost to points of verbal exchange. "Hi, I am Lucy, Dubem's nurse for the day," Lucy said to introduce herself to Isoken. Lucy was an avid lover of science and technology with an unusual liking for mobile gadgets. Tucked away in her scrub pocket was an article on a science magazine that had the caption "Apps Made Easy." Dubem received his Hydrocodone-Acetaminophen pain medication from Lucy who took time to address his other concerns. She could not hide the infatuation from her patient, often patting her hair from her face. Isoken stopped watching TV show and observed the ensuing flirtation.

Dubem asked Lucy if he could take a look at the article that caught his attention. The request came as a pleasant surprise to Lucy; it was a rare opportunity for her. At the corner, Isoken mumbled and hissed like a bicycle pump.

"Some nurses think wearing tight clothing and swinging hips makes an impression," Isoken said to embarrass Lucy. The comment got under Lucy's skin, and she headed for the exit.

Dubem was quick to diffuse the situation. "Pardon her lack of manners," he implored, but it was already too late. He turned toward Isoken with a frightening look.

"You had better restrain yourself from these behaviors and keep all the negative comments to yourself," he demanded.

"Honey, I didn't mean any harm," she said with a calm, unhappy face.

"I need my space," Dubem insisted.

"I'm sorry, Dubem, it's so hard for me to see you flirt with all these beautiful nurses and say nothing," she replied, reaching for her purse and car keys.

Dubem dismissed her claims. "Keep that to yourself."

Reluctant to leave, Isoken asked, "But who's gonna watch over you?"

"I'll be fine for now," he insisted.

A downcast Isoken left for home. If she had the slightest hope that she could rewrite the wrongs, the chances seemed hopeless. Dubem felt justified by his actions because he was pained by her insensitivity toward him in the past weeks.

The next day, the attending's post-discharge instructions were ready. Olivia walked in on Dubem choking from his meal. Quickly, she reached for the head of the bed and raised it; the bed's serial number caught her attention. She shook off the blank stare and handed Dubem a cup of water and observed him till he felt better.

"Sir, I have your discharge instructions, and I'll go over them with you," she said, smiling. "How does that sound?"

"Perfect," he responded with delight. "I am so ready to leave."

"Do you have someone to pick you up, or would you like for us to call you a cab?" she asked.

"That wouldn't be necessary, my friend will come get me," he replied.

Dubem left a voice message for Isoken to pick him up at the hospital's lobby while he packed his belongings. He waited for over four hours, but Isoken never showed up. Lucy and Olivia were headed for the exit and both sighted a dejected-looking figure seated at the corner. Olivia had wheeled her last patient three hours ago, and an hour later, he was still at the lobby. She whispered a few words in Lucy's ear. She was unequivocal with her response to Olivia. "For what it might mean, I will not get into the mix with that wild bitch of his!"

Olivia defied Lucy and walked up to Dubem and asked, "Would you mind if I arrange for a taxi to take you home?"

Dubem was a little embarrassed, but he obliged. "Thanks, I don't mind."

"How far do you stay," she asked.

"About ten minutes from here," he replied.

"Okay, I'll let them know at the reception," she said, walking away.

Dubem arrived at the apartment he shared with Isoken and pretended to search for his wallet.

"Sir, the cab is already paid for," the cabdriver said with a melody to his accent.

The sounds of rattling blinds and the airy living room welcomed him into the apartment—Isoken moved out everything but the air mattress and coffee table. Beneath the coffee mug were a handwritten note and two sheets of yellow-and-pink checkout inventory forms for the apartment complex. The note was a reminder that he'd have to return the forms and the apartment keys six days from the date of the letter. Dubem slid down from the wall to the floor carpet, saddened and helpless with not a fight left in him for the rest of the day. Soon enough, he fell asleep on the floor only to be awakened by the slight morning chill.

Morning meditations were routine, but the abundance of thoughts overwhelmed his calm. Worrying thoughts threatened to hijack his sanity but braced himself up and headed for a quick shower. A sense of calm was restored, and a quick cup of green tea and honey perked him up. The fridge echoed as he opened it—only a few slices of bread and an almost empty bottle of jam stirred him in the face. Far, far away from home, the thought of Monday morning breakfast made him homesick. Halfway sipping his tea, five minutes later, his phone began to ring. Ignoring his mom's call would cause his uncle or aunt to be on the road to Washington, DC, from New Jersey.

"Dubem, what's been going on?"

"Nothing, Mom, I've just been so busy,"

"So busy not to call your mom and dad?"

"For that, I deserved to be spanked," he said, and both laughed.

"I hope you're okay?"

"Yes, Mom, I am," he insisted.

"Anyway, your dad says hello," she said. "Take care of yourself and don't forget that Mom loves you."

Dubem sat on the couch, contemplating his next move; suddenly, the pages of the tech magazine which he got from Lucy flipped open by his side. The opened page was an article which talked about steps to create an app and how it could change people's lives. By the time he realized it, he had finished reading the article twice; everything about the article seemed practical and believable—he was sold in on it. He turned on his mobile hot spot and laptop, searching for resources on how to build an app.

*****

Four days before the lease expired, the drive to succeed at all costs was intense. Most of the days were spent in the Library of Congress flipping through books. Tireless work meant fewer bathroom breaks; he had no business idling about the library's ambiance.

Samantha, a self-styled freelance journalist, observed Dubem's work ethics with keen interest. She had a rebellious streak about her appearance: a side-shave to her hair, nose and finger rings, and black lipstick. Like Dubem, she was an only child who opted to lead her life the way she wanted, except one thing: get engaged to Bruce Keller who was a top-aspiring prosecutor in her parents' law firm. Samantha had to choose between this love match or forget freelancing. Becoming a freelance journalist was against the behest of her parents, Kathy and Donald Milford. Aside the preference of arguing cases in the courtrooms, both parents wanted her to take over their successful law firm in the district. To her, he was a jerk of a man and had no ounce of love for him. Frequently, she was reminded about the poor choice she made by passing up the offer at Princeton Law School to become a freelancer. Sometimes, these misunderstandings got the better of her, and she gave herself one more year to give freelance a try.

The next day, Samantha was at the Library of Congress and saw Dubem seated at the same spot. After one of his bathroom breaks, she walked curiously behind his table to peek at what he was working on. Dubem had a spooky feeling, and Samantha's citrusy fragrance swept by from the closing door, then he looked back.

"I'm sorry for sneaking up on you," she implored. "My name is Samantha Milford."

"Dubem Okoli," he said, extending a handshake.

"Seems an interesting drawing you've got going on that paper?" she asked.

Dubem chuckled. "Quite interesting, indeed," he affirmed.

"Do you do this every day?" she asked. "I mean study here…"

"Not exactly," he responded. "I'm quite fascinated with app developments."

"Don't tell me this is one of those 'pastime' hobbies?" she asked.

"You could say that," Dubem said with a smile.

"You're just plain ole geeky," she teased.

Samantha tried not to murder his name so she came up with something close.

"Duby, we could talk more about this over brunch tomorrow," she suggested. "On my on tabs."

Dubem thought of the only $50 to his name but was relieved it was not his to spend, so he accepted the offer.

Later that day, beautiful memories Dubem once held of the apartment shrunk by the minute, even the air mattress progressively deflated. Most, if not all, he lived on was Chinese food, which he rationed. Long and hard he thought into the early hours of the morning; still unsure of the future, he held on for another day.

Dubem met up with Samantha for brunch as planned, and they had a few minutes of hearty laughter before the important conversations.

"So why freelance journalism?" Dubem asked.

Samantha sighed. "Long story."

"You could start from somewhere," Dubem suggested.

"Well, my parents own a successful law firm and have always wanted a successor," she said. "But I am not cut out for it."

"Says who?" Dubem asked unapologetically.

"Don't get me wrong, I got accepted to Princeton Law School." She sighed. "Law is not just for me."

"You really are a weird one," he said dismissively.

She was about to end the brunch abruptly, but he pleaded his cause; they switched focus a moment.

"So you do know a thing about following your heart?" she asked, looking intrigued.

"My girlfriend gave up on me because I tried to follow it," he said, looking away.

Samantha reached for his hand on the table. "Duby, you're not alone 'coz I'm not in love with the bloke my parents forced on me."

Dubem seemed surprised to hear that her love was matchmade, something not associated with America. Despite Dubem's insistence on paying part of the bill before leaving, Samantha refused to accept his offer for it was her treat.

Samantha was taken aback by the extent to which she opened up to Dubem, but it felt good talking to a reasonable man other than Bruce. Unusually, the moment she spent with Dubem conveyed positivity, and it was irresistibly attractive. Closing hours for the library could not come any faster. Samantha hurriedly packed her laptop and writing materials fast enough to catch up with her brunch buddy.

Dubem was aloof to his surroundings but was surprised to hear his name called from across the street. Samantha hurried over to the other side of the road to his position.

"Hey, are you walking, driving, or catching the train?"

Dubem sighed. "I really don't know," he said.

"Come along, I'll give you a ride home," she insisted.

Samantha observed Dubem's stare aimlessly outside the window, and she knew something bothered him. No matter how he tried to mask it, he was never one to pretend unless it absolutely mattered.

"Tell me what's on your mind," she insisted.

"Trust me, you don't want to be bothered," he said, trying to talk Samantha out of it.

"Life no longer surprises me," she responded with a shrug.

"By this time tomorrow, I'd be without a home," he said with sadness.

Samantha didn't think through it for a second and was quick to respond. "Not a problem, you can stay in my uncle Lenny's house," she suggested. "He sublets his house when on sea with the US Navy."

"Wow! You're a life saver I'll reach out to you if I run out of options," he said with a tone of appreciation.

*****

Several thoughts crossed Dubem's mind as he tried to fall asleep twenty-four hours before the move-out deadline.

So beneath the Gothic look, her true spirit comes alive: real, unpretentious, and free-spirited. Every day she shows me another side of her... but then if I brought her to Mom and Dad, they'd think I've lost it. I think I'm falling for her.

As soon as he was about to shut his eyes, Isoken called. He looked at the phone and thought it to be rather odd. It wouldn't cost him a thing to find out the reason for this call.

"Yes, Isoken," he said. "What do you want from me now?"

"Do you have a place to stay?"

"No, I have not, but I'll be fine." he replied. "Isoken, is this your own idea of ridiculing me?"

He thought for a second to tell her about Samantha's offer, but it didn't matter to him anyway. Isoken was silent for a minute, probably searching her soul to act accordingly, then she returned to the conversation.

"Have your suitcase ready, I'll be there early tomorrow morning to get you," she said before hanging up.

Dubem couldn't quite comprehend Isoken's erratic nature, let alone understand her thought process. Sure enough, Isoken was early that morning to pick him up.

For the next four weeks, Dubem put up with Isoken in her town house. He had no money to his name, so he was mindful of friction. In between, he resorted to odd-paying jobs: walking and grooming dogs for an old couple three blocks from Isoken's house. On his way back from returning the dogs, he took a hard look within…

I have crossed the vast expanse of the Atlantic. What has become of me, a man walking dogs for a living? My value is worth more than neither pennies nor dollars. I am a thoroughbred with an unusual path, an unusual purpose. Oh, spirit of mine, arise with utmost conviction for my road must lead me to the treasures my heart seeks…I have willed, the gods must obey!

Isoken's late nights and harangues epitomized Dubem's extra four weeks at hers. Slowly, Dubem was becoming despondent, but he kept spirits up with his app design. Thankfully, Samantha provided a valuable escape from reality. What hurt Dubem the most was how quickly Isoken forgot who shared her highs and lows while chasing success in her undergraduate and master's program. Who could forget those cold, dark nights where willpower was elusive and the pep talk of a loving cheerleader crucial? So quickly Isoken forgot the nights he combed through journals brainstorming while she took well-deserved naps. Indeed, looking back at those nights could usher in bitterness but never regrets.

*****

Straight through the quiet hours of the night, Samantha brainstormed with Dubem on a few issues regarding the app at her uncle

Lenny's house. He created a wire frame prototype of his app and added the graphical component to the story board. The app is intended to measure in real time levels of sodium, potassium, chloride, bicarbonate, blood urea nitrogen, creatinine, glucose, etc. from a tincture of blood sample. In addition, the app would have the capacity to chart results over a period, provide risk analysis and possible diagnoses, and, most importantly, transmit the lab result within seconds to an individual's primary care physician.

A few unforeseen glitches arose, and Samantha swung into action, calling upon her childhood friend, Yoshi Takayasu, a computer programming genius. For fun, he would take apart even the smallest device, decipher its algorithm and rewrite or modify the program. Dubem described the concept of attaching the measuring device to a smartphone to Yoshi, and he was up and running. Yoshi was satisfied after inspecting the app's frame and component story. Next, he pulled from his tool bag a small, racquet-like device with a pin plug and attached it to a device by the port of his computer. When asked what it was, Yoshi said that it was a smart glucometer device that he found along a computer junk site while he was vacationing in Tokyo. With the device recognized by his laptop, his fingers bounced off the keyboards in rapid succession, inputting codes every step of the way. Within a few seconds, he coupled Dubem's app algorithm with the existing one on the glucometer device—something they never could have imagined. Right before Samantha and Dubem's eyes, the device was now able to check an individual's glucose, electrolytes, and basic metabolic panels; they called this device iPanels.

To see if it the app worked as it should, it required a live test, as well as test strips. Samantha was up for the ride—off she drove to the nearest twenty-four-hour pharmacy store and purchased a box of glucose test strips. Midway through the drive back, Bruce called to remind her about the court wedding in Tucson, Arizona, in two days. The news should have been a happy one; instead, it dampened her spirit. She returned with the strips, and Dubem was given the honors to be pricked with the lancet. As Dubem cringed, he noticed Samantha's countenance change, but the excitement and the pain from the prick shifted his focus albeit momentarily. Yoshi inserted the strip into the smart glucometer device and took a sample of Dubem's blood. Now the real test was moments away. Yoshi slotted the device into the port of the smartphone. A "Result Analysis" dialogue box popped up on the screen; he tapped the prompt, and everyone held their breath. There it was—a detailed analysis of glucose, electrolytes, and basic metabolic panel values were on full display. Ecstasy was written all over their faces!

On their drive back to Isoken's house, Dubem probed Samantha for answers to her sudden look hours ago. She did an awful job of trying to hide her emotions. After much ado, she opened up to him and swore this was not her making. At Isoken's driveway, Dubem alighted from the car deflated. She waited for him to enter the house.

"I see you've got yourself another weirdo, a rock star," Isoken said with a calm tone.

"Her name is Samantha," he clarified. "She is a freelance journalist, not a rock star."

"Well, whatever you say," she said sarcastically. "I'm afraid you'd have to leave my house…"

Dubem turned toward her in shock. "You joke a lot," he said.

"This time, Dubem, I am not joking," she said. "You'll find $500 in an envelope to cover any inconveniences."

He dragged his feet to the room to meet an already packed suitcase. It was the lowest he could be, but a strange wind of confidence stirred up within as he walked back to the living room.

"For all the love I have given, I don't deserve this treatment," he said with a sad voice. Isoken pretended to be on the phone—or so it seemed. Dubem placed a call to Samantha who for some reason refused to leave the driveway. Perhaps she drifted off while she loathed life's cruelties.

Before departing, he said, "Isoken, I'm grateful for all you've done and for all the hard times we've shared. I'm sorry, I was not the man you hoped for. Hard times never last, this I believe." He reiterated, "I love you, and I wish you everything good in life."

Dubem loaded his suitcase and bag into the waiting car. Isoken went into the room and saw the envelope that she placed on top of his suitcase. He refused to be insulted even in his desperate state. Isoken was full of regrets afterward.

It was a quiet drive back to uncle Lenny's house, and Samantha cuddled the night away with Dubem. Once the sun was up, Dubem looked to the other side of the room, and Samantha stood looking at him with a teary eyes and red face.

"I have to go now," she said. "I owe my fleeting joy to you," she said.

It was apparent to him that he was about to lose another companion. Surely, he dreaded this conversation and wanted it to be quick.

"Samantha, I know, and I understand," he said.

"But I promise you, Duby, I owe you one," she said with tears trickling down her face. "You can stay till when you find a place and mail the keys to me."

Despite the summer sunshine, Dubem stayed indoors for the rest of the day, pondering over the unfolding tales of his young adult life.

*****

Dubem came up with a plan the next morning to get a doctor's visit at Providence Hospital. Soon enough, he placed a call to his doctor's office hoping to get a walk-in visit for "periodic weakness" as chief complaint. He was lucky: one of the scheduled patients was a no-show. The doctor preferred the hospital's lab because the results were accessible to patients via a secured web portal on the same day. So he ordered a comprehensive lab panel for Dubem slip to the hospital's lab. On his way out, he bumped into Olivia. She saw him first and tried to avoid him, but the reaction time was short. Dubem exchanged pleasantries and attempted to walk in the opposite direction. The picture that played in Olivia's mind was that of a stranded lad, and she felt compelled to help.

"Wait a minute, are you headed in the direction of Michigan Avenue?" she asked.

"Not really," he said, "but I live about two miles from here."

"That's not bad," she replied. "Come along, I can get you there."
"You are so kind, thanks a lot!" he said, looking relieved.

Conversations were congenial throughout the ride, and Dubem was not sure how he missed this pleasant beauty while at the hospital. Those rose-colored cheekbones and her well-defined facial structures were all the more alluring. True to her words, she waited for Dubem to get the test done. On their drive back, Dubem briefed Yoshi about the app updates and asked to meet up with him at uncle Lenny's house within an hour. The conversation though short was detailed, so she was patient for him to get off the phone and ask questions. Olivia wanted to understand the app's benefits. Dubem anticipated the question and he explained it to her admiration.

"It's designed to capture your glucose, electrolyte panels, and more in real time. The in-built algorithms helps one decide if a condition is emergent or requires you to send a copy to a doctor or see a doctor. One cool feature is that it gives you a list of possible medical conditions that may relate to abnormal values."

"In essence, you're improving health outcomes, right?" Olivia asked. "That's innovative!"

"You bet it does," Dubem said and winked at her epiphany. "Yoshi is coming over so we can compare the results of iPanels with the traditional lab results." Olivia proposed lunch for the next day at her place and Dubem could not pass up the offer.

Before Yoshi would arrive, Olivia stepped away to fix Dubem a cup of coffee and lunch at her place. As soon as Olivia returned to the living room, Munchkeen seemed overly excited and went into strange displays.

"I'm so sorry, I have never seen him act like this with a visitor," Olivia said, looking confused.

"It's okay, he doesn't bother me one bit," he replied with a cautious smile.

At the living room, Dubem deliberated on where he had seen the dog while Olivia was at the kitchen losing patience over Munchkeen's weird displays. As she made her way to the living room with two cups of coffee, Munchkeen ran between her legs and jumped onto Dubem's laps and snatched his cell phone.

"Get down and out, little brat!" Olivia yelled, but Munchkeen had other plans. With the cell phone between his jaws, he jumped down and sat by the couch with one paw on the screen.

Suddenly, a warm touch rested upon her shoulders and felt the hairs on her skin rise. When she looked at Dubem, she recalled the hospital bed's serial number; next, the image of the handwritten note in the trinket box flashed in her mind's eye. The voice that followed the image was soft and crystal clear: "We are blind because we chose not to see, we are deaf because we chose not to hear. We fail to see the future because we ignore the present."

Olivia was frightened, and the coffee cups dropped from her hands to the floor, which startled Munchkeen. Dubem hurried to help, but Olivia departed his presence faster than he could reach her. Everything felt strange and confusing to Dubem. Ten minutes later, Olivia returned just in time when Yoshi called Dubem, then she drove him to Uncle Lenny's house.

For a final test run, Yoshi coupled the device that had Dubem's blood sample and slotted it into the laptop's port; then, he tapped the prompt to display the results. The wait was nerve-wracking. Yoshi's fist pump signaled a new dawn—both results were almost identical in values before the screen went blank! Dubem and Yoshi looked at each other: it was the timely intervention of the surge protector. At this moment, Dubem began to make sense of the strange happenings that trailed his path while he was in a coma.

*****

Samantha's article gained massive viewership in medical and tech blogs the day iPanels was patented. Dubem and Yoshi never expected the picture collage Samantha shared, which chronicled the stages of the app's development. A plethora of calls as well as bookings flooded Samantha's e-mail and social media pages, offering her all manner of gigs.

Dubem flew Samantha in to Washington, DC, for the brunch he owed her. Thanks to the trust fund of Olivia's mother that helped secure a prototype model for a patent. Fortune smiled kindly on

Dubem even further. On one of Olivia's lunch breaks at the hospital, an excited Dubem was seen at the lobby with an iPanel prototype, explaining in details to Olivia. Seated across from them was the vice chair of the John's Hopkins Board of Trustees, who incidentally stumbled across Samantha's article a week prior. The mildly mannered vice chair left his business card with Dubem.

At the beginning of fall that year, John's Hopkins Hospital bought the exclusive rights to the iPanels, and the preliminary data and benefits that trailed the first quarter launch of the app were positive—in fact, beyond belief!

End

SUGAR PALAVER

Every generation must recognize and embrace the task it is peculiarly designed by history and by providence to perform.

—Chinua Achebe

September

Even in the grimmest of times, the years preceding 1996 were a beehive of activities at Bamenda Locomotive (BL) Ltd. A sizeable number of traders—largely Igbos from Eastern Nigeria—trooped in from neighboring Douala and Yaoundé to patronize BL. Aloysius "Aloy" Mbafout's prosperity was no fluke—what BL had become was testament to sheer sweat and willpower. Among other money spinners, his transport automobile rental business was the most viable commercially, especially the months before Christmas and the New Year: September through November. It all changed when power-wielding officials, fueled by greed, pitted brothers against friends.

Bamenda's glowing reputation for hospitality was denigrated by a few unscrupulous men at the helm of affairs. Like smoke, rumors were rife about the impending levies, but the unimaginative hands of many stoked the fire that shook the city. Reckless slurs deepened fault lines, stares turned menacing, and bottle-breaking fisticuffs settled old scores. Movement was restricted, and the streets had become inhospitable for the Igbo traders who responded pound for pound.

Over the years, the lush Bamenda grasslands metamorphosed into an expansive region of commercial activities, and human settlements still dotted with harbingers of its colonial past. Bamenda City's market was not all about work and jive; it had its own fair share of tales and woes. The life span of a business was never guaranteed, but some outlived others. Traders clung to religion for good fortunes. But for Aloy, on the contrary, he was an eternal optimist. If any oracle had the slightest confidence in his or her ability, when it came to Aloy, they were cautious enough to avoid making inaccurate declarations—for he was an *enfant terrible* in matters of business. Many had tried to outwit him in the past but failed.

One prediction that left an impression in the minds of Bamenda traders (three years prior) was that of the "Apostle" as he was fondly called. Apostle had other names: divine minister, general overseer, and grand commander of the Charismatic Prayer Warriors of the Cameroons. On a particular day, he went about preaching and prophesying, driven around in a rickety, metallic blue Peugeot station wagon before settling across from BL. Apostle emerged headfirst from the windowless door, clasped his megaphone in his right hand, and sat on the door panel. The melancholic tunes blaring from the boulder-sized speakers on top of the car suddenly went silent. He proclaimed, "Before the month of October, I see the enemy drowning you in a pool of blood…your victory in this message rests on special prayers and consultations I offer!" (April 26, 1993).

Apostle's prophecy traversed the hinterlands like gusty desert winds. It seemed as though it left its inhabitants confused about the prophecy as different versions of it emerged. The resultant implications and interpretations of the prophecy were overarching and, at best, extreme. The foretold prophecy wore the cloak of misery: it was a source of companionship among the gatherings of men and, on the other hand, perched on the glib-lipped women in marketplaces. Sinister tales, by some accounts, claimed to have seen vultures gather around a mysterious campfire at night under a palm tree at the back of Aloy's fenced house, patiently waiting to sample the flesh from his carcass. Such extrapolation of tales never fazed him, for he had seen and heard all sorts as an experienced businessman. Nonetheless October 1993 came along, and not a scintilla of proclamation manifested. Quietly, Apostle retreated into the recess of the "mountain."

From dusk to dawn, ardent followers kept vigil for Apostle's arrival. Days turned into weeks, and weeks to months, still not a glimpse of Apostle. While devoted followers kept hope alive with persistent prayers at vigils, fair-weather sycophants slipped through the ranks with one eye fixed at the exit door. The ministry was fast slipping into oblivion. Dangling from the gates of the ministry was a sign that read thus: Journeyed to the Wilderness.

*****

Bamenda Locomotive (BL), 8:22 a.m., October, day one

It was Thursday—the last day of the month—when Aloy glanced at his watch. His robust frame rose from the office chair and walked toward the side of the office entrance overlooking the adjoining street. Bored stiff, he stood there for a few seconds, took a breath of fresh air, and scanned the vicinity in one fell swoop. Aloy marveled at the view. The swarming activities of the market never gave him the opportunity to see the market's outline; Bamenda City's market had come a long way. Aloy stroked one of two pillars beneath the fancy arch projections from the entrance of BL with admiration. To his left sat a tall, three-legged stool, which one of his trainees probably left behind before leaving on an errand. With the stool in both hands, he contemplated an ideal position to place it. When he drifted away from awareness, his innermost chatter attained a voice of its own—sometimes to his chagrin.

Which kin' problem be this? Why human beings no fit live in peace? We no fit appreciate the thing we get until we lose am. Na we provoke them to go strike, them lockup shop. Why city council begin disturb Igbo people for levy for God's sake?

The atmosphere outside held two contrasting views: one burdened with emotions and the other simplicity. Plaintive gospel melodies in the background searched his soul. In spite of the somber atmosphere, the dusty Harmattan winds dispersed its fair share of silt; gyrating coffee-colored leaves hung in midair before settling on the ground. Every passing minute betrayed the desolate state of a once-lively market. But gradually, Aloy's state of apathy triggered a shift down memory lane as his gaze settled on the hilly uptown district in the distance. His memory served him, a trickle at a time, images long buried in his subconsciousness.

*****

Time flies, it really does. At fifteen years old, Aloy was already street-smart, but no upbringing or business acumen was sufficient enough to prepare him for his apprenticeship at Obioma & Sons Enterprise, Onitsha, Nigeria. As a naive teenager, he was adventurous and daring to think that the outside world would fetch the desires of his heart on a platter of gold. Reality may not have been far from the truth.

Aloy pondered, *Onitsha market was the busiest I had ever seen, human and automobile traffic competed for the slightest of space. Yet in the midst of all this chaos, I saw a pattern to the madness. My Igbo friends, I wonder what has become of you all? Where would I have been if it were not for your help? Perhaps I would have been harassed and homeless. Or do I forget so easily my first job at Obioma & Sons Enterprise? Oh, how sad and petrified I was during the senseless war. I cursed the day the Nigerian Army's 2ⁿᵈ Division made landfall in Onitsha despite the dogged resistance of the Biafran Army's 11ᵗʰ, 12ᵗʰ, and 18ᵗʰ Battalions. It was the most frightening experience of my youth: bombs dropped like rain from the skies, bullets smashing through glass doors and windows— missing my chin by a whisker. My good friends feared for my safety. I had become part of them. I shared their pain, I ran every race for dear life, but my good friends looked after me. Mr. Obioma needed it more, but in the hardest of times, he made me sixty pounds and twenty shillings richer. It was his parting gift to me, an investment for my future. It was the last I saw of him. Onitsha was no longer safe as the federal troops rolled in, plundering and incinerating the once vibrant market. Ozoemena, the older brother I never had, whisked me on his back, navigating through rugged terrains to the border, just in time for the last bus to Bamenda. Tears rolled down my cheeks. I was not prepared to let go of my embrace—yes, I was selfish—but he knew it was the best for me. It was hard for him too. He looked up to the heavens, let out a huge sigh, and ran off into the bushes…*

*****

November, day two

The first day of the month did not change much from the previous day. Business was snail-paced, and Aloy was out again for some fresh air. From the adjoining street, to the right of BL, Jules fixed his eyes on his boss, Aloy, who sat in front of the office's entrance. Two days in a row, he observed his boss lost in his own world. He thought of the present impasse in Bamenda. So far gone was he that he hardly knew when, Jules, his bookkeeper sneaked up beside him.

"*Oga* Aloy, everything good?" he asked. Jules's raspy voice shook Aloy such that he almost lost his footing.

"*Na* you this!" Aloy sighed. "Since they make Igbo people lock-up shop, business come slow. *Wetin* man *pikin* go do?"

Jules concurred. "*Na* true talk be that, *oga.*"

After ruminating over the plight of the masses, he asked for an up-to-date transaction log. Ordinarily, what he requested of Jules was what Kenechukwu "Kene" Ibe, the store manager, would have provided. The solidarity among the Igbo Traders Union (ITU), which Kene was part of, made it all the more frustrating for Aloy to judge his company's monthly earnings; nonetheless, he understood the importance of trade unions. Kene was Aloy's "second" eye, wielding all the authority hitherto. Many times, the workers groused at the unprecedented trust that Aloy had in this so-called Awala man (generally ascribed to Nigerians living in Cameroon). Kene's status was elevated further when Aloy read the riot act, which refrained workers from making sly remarks toward his trusted manager. Consequently, they could only resort to snickering surreptitiously. There was little wonder why he was elevated to a status of a demigod. Aside Kene, Jules knew it was in the Awala man's country he learned the ropes of trading and management that changed his life for the better. For this, he remained eternally grateful. Jules brought the logbook for his boss's perusal; he stood elbow-length behind his boss and clasped his hands at his back. He prayed fervently and hoped he wouldn't see the "Balance Brought Forward" section. Irrespective of profit, Aloy still paid attention to his company's bottom line: a shrewd businessman personified.

"Jules!" Aloy repeated three times.

"Yes, *masa?*" he replied. When Jules heard his name called more than once, he knew the signs were ominous.

"Why you no tell me say Patrice never pay for the three motor since March? And you come rent am for November again…eh?" Aloy asked.

At this point, Jules had his tail between his legs; he wished the ground beneath could swallow him. "*Masa*, it is devil work," he replied.

Upon hearing his response, Aloy turned swiftly. "*Wetin* you talk!"

When Jules saw his boss's bloodshot eyes, he lost all courage to respond.

"Okay, I go cut half your money for three months. Devil go balance you the rest!"

*****

Mankon town was home to the most reviled underground racketeering kingpin, Patrice Elangwe; that was in his heyday, but he turned a new leaf after amassing a substantial amount of monies. From a distance, Patrice had a lot of disdain for Aloy for several reasons. Patrice's mother, on numerous occasions, compared his life's trajectory to that of Aloy's and derided him for being improvident and unambitious. To make matters worse, he could not stand the fact that Aloy trusted an Awala man to oversee his business above a Cameroonian-run business.

Ill-gotten wealth without proper planning and investment is nothing but a flash in a saucepan—or at best, water draining from a basket. Patrice's case was no exception. In the last year or two, his resources began to dwindle, so he had to look for an alternative to sustain cash flow. Consequently, he resorted to mini Ponzi schemes in neighboring villages and towns all in the guise of youth empowerment. Strangely, they were run by men in their twenties with specific characteristics: no formal education, muscular, and of athletic build. During the ITU strike, Patrice saw an opportunity.

The citizens of Mankon town took for granted the business savviness of their visitors. It was well-known that the Igbo traders—hate or like them—had a major say in the sale of bare necessities, which they called "provisions." Among these provisions, sugar was like "white gold." Families and food vendors alike felt the impact of sugarless meals and French-inspired gourmets. What sold for ten Central African CFA franc (CFA francs) per kilo had risen to fifty CFA francs per kilo within the space of two days. Patrice had bought over all the sugar supplies from petty traders at the initial price and sold it at four times the price. Fortuitously, the pickup vans he had rented from BL on credit came in handy. On several occasions, his bulky-looking foot soldiers hurled a generous amount of bags of sugar into the waiting van. People who matched his accomplices' bravado eyeball-for-eyeball were seen hopping on crutches days later.

*****

Day two to four

Meanwhile, the contentious atmosphere in Bamenda City reached a fever pitch. Demonstrations by traders, the insensitivity of the head of the Urban City Council, and the heavy-handedness of the gendarmeries on both citizens and immigrants were loaded canons, waiting to unleash mayhem. Every effort by the citizenry to reach the head of the city council proved abortive. Instead, traders and sundry were sent on a wild goose chase for answers.

Brigadier General Aruna Bagaleh was the then head of the army division to whom Colonel Bede Mfon reported to concerning matters of civil unrest. All branches were under the aegis of the Ministry of Defense (MOD). It was widely perceived—but unspoken—that Lt. Col. Constantine Mesoumbe was the secret shield of Patrice. The coded working relationship was no doubt tainted with bribery: a byword shrouded in the loins of absolute power. This secret partnership ensured not only Constantine's regular kickbacks but espoused Patrice's brigandage during the ongoing crises.

Word had reached the president regarding the level of unrest, and the president's demand was absolute: restore order with immediate alacrity! Likewise, the minister of defense's response was swift. Summarily, Gen. Aruna, Col. Bede, and Lt. Col. Constantine were summoned to the MOD. Depending on who told the story, gossip that filtered out was that the minister descended heavily on his subjects. His action was likened to the treatment meted out by Fon Garega—as narrated by Eugene Zintgraff—to his "unpunctual sub-chiefs." Aruna, Bede, and Constantine were given twenty-four hours to restore order, but that was a subliminal way of telling them to prepare for redeployment.

The second day after the meeting, a signal was sent by the army headquarters for both men to report for further debriefing. The actions that followed were rapid, resulting in a change of guard. The redeployed officers, on the basis of hierarchy, were succeeded by their deputies: Lt. Col. Madakey Tatcho (for Col. Bede) and Maj. Pierre Nshome (for Lt. Col. Constantine), respectively. Madakey and Nshome brimmed with audacity: they set out on a pugilistic mission, leaving the errant few with bloodied noses. Whenever common sense failed to prevail, reprobates were slammed in through the back doors of the Black Maria (police van).

*****

Day five

Back in BL, six days had passed since the beginning of the strike, and because Aloy had other expansion projects running concurrently, the ongoing strike was ill-timed. The enormous financial involvements and the payment of worker's salaries took its toll. If Aloy stood any chance to sustain the pace of the ongoing projects, he had to maintain income streams at all costs. Time was of the essence.

Aloy pondered his next move in his office. He reclined on his chair and lifted both legs atop the edge of his table. The competing sounds of the ticking clock at the top-left corner of his office wall and the squeaky white fan on the ceiling went in and out of harmony as his thoughts wandered. He felt that the Igbo traders had been taken advantage of for far too long just like his people in the south. If anyone knew better what it meant for a people to feel marginalized and betrayed by a country, it would be his associate, Ejiofor, fearless and indomitable! Another problem that bothered Aloy was Patrice's debt of seven hundred thousand CFA francs, which meant a lot because it affected his company's financial bottom line.

In the cause of introspection, he also thought of persuading Patrice to pay his past due balance or perhaps send a sales boy to him. On another note, he felt meeting him in person would secure a prompt payment of his debt. Aloy deliberated upon these two thoughts, but whatever the case may be, he was determined to retrieve the money. Rising from this reclined position, he pressed a button by his desk, and the bell rang. Salomon, more often than not, arrived before any staff; he walked sprightly and possessed the energy of a horse—just the right man for the errand. Aloy instructed Salomon to inform Ejiofor to arrive at his abode an hour before midnight. Off Salomon went, leaving the trailing dust behind.

*****

Mankon town

Ten minutes before 11:00 p.m., the floodlights at Aloy's residence went off, but a few odd lights in the house were left on. Ejiofor prepared to leave Aloy's residence at Mankon town without the full glare of the security floodlights capable of illuminating a soccer stadium. It was an oddity around the neighborhood as a few outdoor relaxation dens relied on the radiant beams at no cost. One person whose thoughts went beyond the idea of coincidence was a lady named Madame "Ma" Belle, dubbed "Radio du Bamenda." Shutting off the floodlights meant more to her than just an excuse for an electrical mishap. She had to know why, of course.

Four hours prior to the blackout, she walked past a tall figure whose strut was confident and awe-inspiring. (Judging from his well-trimmed facial hair, she guessed he was in his fifties.) On typical days, Ma Belle flared like a peacock whenever she knew eyes were on her, but this fellow destabilized her composure—she genuflected before realizing it. In return, his nod was measured. For reasons unknown—be it infatuation, lust, or otherwise—Belle was both anxious and curious; she wished to know the significance of this august visitor. Predictably, she tarried on the fringes of Aloy's vicinity for hours, shuffling between hurriedly put-together entertainment dens across the road.

Before long, the entrance gate to Aloy's residence screeched open. The farewell exchange between Aloy and his guest was brief. Ejiofor adjusted the weight on his motorbike and pushed it a few meters away from the gate, started his ignition, and sped off into the dark. He rode westward in the opposite direction of the half-cast moon and veered off the road after two hundred yards. This change in direction was purely strategic because as an ex-guerrilla, he learned to leave nothing to chance. Little did he know he was not as elusive as he imagined. Fortunately for Ejiofor, it was difficult for the prowler to make out what was on the bike.

*****

Day six to nine

Two days passed. Ma Belle could only help but brood over the word—*la resistance*. From what she understood, one only needed to embellish English words with nasal and vocal gags to derive their

French equivalent. It dawned on her that "resistance" had to relate one way or another to "opposition." Ma Belle had a cordial relationship with Patrice, who knew her worth, so it was only natural for her to go to him.

In no time, Ma Belle arrived at Patrice's residence to relay what transpired forty-eight hours ago. She pounded the gate so hard that it disturbed Patrice from devouring his late lunch. He gnashed his teeth, stared at his gate and back at his meal. Reluctantly, he left his steaming yellow soup floating atop a volcanic, craterlike mound of *achu* (pounded cocoyam).

"That person *wey* dey knock for gate suppose get better tin to talk or else thunder go fire him whole generation," he said.

Ma Belle saw the stare on Patrice's face as the gate swung inward.

"Pa, no worry. I just talk say make I come salute you," she mumbled. "This your yard *don* fine well," she said. "I never see this *kin'* flowers for here so."

Patrice cleared his throat and wiped his right hand over the cloth around his waist.

"Pa, the way you stand so be like say you no wan' make I enter."

"*Na* story for help we all for *paye?*" His shoulders slowly dropped, and his eyes looked curious, then he ushered her in.

After he served her fresh palm wine and a few pieces of spicy goat meat, Ma Belle never paused until she uttered the last words. She narrated how Ejiofor stealthily departed Aloy's residence, meandering his way into the dark via dirt roads. By her estimation, Ejiofor had departed with a sack-load of cash to the tune of a few million CFAs. When asked how she came about the figures, she opined that Ejiofor's wobbled gait was unmistakable in the full glare of the moonlit skies.

To Patrice's chagrin, via other sources, he learned later on that the covert movement of cash was an ongoing plot for the proliferation of arms to the Southern People's Ambazonia Militia (SPAM). Left to him, Aloy committed the highest treason for secretly funding the agitation for the self-determination of the people of southern Cameroons from La République. Before Patrice became fully aware of this plot, popular opinions previously dismissed such information as a mere myth. Insofar as the brewing insecurity concerns remained a myth, it granted the orchestrators of the secession movement laissez-passer.

*****

Day ten, at the MOD

The following day, Patrice arrived at the office of the gendar-merie to see his friend. Major Nshome was reading through his daily security briefings and assessing levels of threat when he heard a knock on his door. Before he could adjust, the door opened swiftly. Nshome had seen that type of expression on Patrice's face before—a furrow over his brow, biting his lips.

He motioned. "*Assieds-toi! Q'est que c'est* problem?"

"Idiot!" was all Nshome heard from the door till he took his seat.

"Calm down, my friend," said the major.

"Ah, *mon frère*, snake *don* hide for on top plantain tree!"

Nshome dropped the briefs on the incoming receptacle, and his chair screeched closer to the table.

"Make you tell me quick, quick. I no get time for hear proverb!" said Nshome.

"That Awala man *pikin* carry money give some people make them fight we," said Patrice.

"How you take know?" Nshome asked.

"That one no matter, *mon frère*," Patrice replied dismissively. "She no fit give me wrong information. Anything she talk, *mon frère*, *na* true talk!" he exclaimed.

Angrily, Nshome reached for a button to the right of his desk. The relentless clapping of the bell sent a corporal and a sergeant scrambling through Nshome's office door—that was seconds before the bell's fuse blew. Both of them ducked on hearing the loud noise, but the corporal was first to react as he attempted to make a round-about dash for the door from which he arrived.

"*Arrêtez là*! Where you for go?"

"Sir, I want to check whether it is gun," he saluted.

"You think say I dey joke?"

"No, sir!" both replied while standing at attention.

Nshome looked up and yelled, "Sergeant! Where for this report you talk about *la resistance*?

The sergeant looked to his right at the corporal in search of a clue, and the corporal shook his head in disbelief.

"Answer me, Sergeant!"

"*Oga*, I never hear about am before," he replied.

Nshome could not believe how lax the force had become for a superior officer to receive a report before his subordinates were unheard of. Next, he ordered a full-scale investigation that was due to him within seventy-two hours. He did not have to say much. The junior rank and files knew the outcome of not delivering.

With Nshome and Patrice now alone, the two of them thought of ways to nullify the uprising: first for national interest and second for other reasons best known to them.

*****

Day eleven, Bamenda Locomotive

By the following day, word reached Philemon Ndefi (field commander of SPAM) that funds for the procurement of assault weaponry were in transit. Included in the veiled message was a three-phase master plan for the actualization of the underground movement toward self-determination. Before that time, the SPAM movement was merely conceptual, but Ejiofor's involvement gave it life. Other pressing issues required his attention, so he switched focus from the brewing disenchantment on the other side of the divide toward the ongoing ITU strike. Several meetings were held at his behest with his trusted allies taken into confidence regarding the impending doom ahead, and all resolved to play the ostrich.

A week after the covert meeting that transpired in Mankon town, Aloy anticipated feedback. Ingeniously, his antiestablishment posture went unnoticed by his staff. Needless to say, every discussion held or any association with key actors in the movement had to be shrouded in secrecy, not even his staff could be trusted.

It was a lunch break at BL, and the staff—in their usual boisterous mood—where exhilarated about the game of checkers they were playing. Separated by the playing board, two contestants (players) sat across from each other while five others formed a circle around them. At times like these, smack-talking individuals settled bloodless scores. No matter how many jibes the competitors hurled at each other, in the end, it was all part of the show and love for the game. As easy as it sounds, nobody wanted to be on the losing end.

Amid all the cheers and jeers, two strangers arrived at BL half a minute apart; they requested to see Aloy. The first one was cordial and posed as a sugar mill business owner in need of a distributor, and in no time he was ushered in to see their boss. But the one who arrived last wore a mean look and offered nothing but monosyllabic responses when questioned. His protruding pectoralis and the engorged veins running across his arms had the staff at BL looking over their shoulders at the slightest sound of shuffling feet.

"Where your *oga*?" the stranger asked. The slight pause felt like an eternity, and then he followed up with, "All of you no get ears?" he asked.

It was difficult for the staff (in the middle of a game) to produce an answer. Perhaps the slew of thoughts running through their minds was nerve-racking. Thoughts of a hired assassin or an unscrupulous thug were not far from the ordinary.

The stranger scanned his peripheral view, and in one swift move, clutched the neck of Salomon from the back, and the rest of the staff dispersed in all directions. Almost all of Salomon's neck was holed up in his huge palms save for a few inches from his thyroid cartilage.

Gasping for air, Salomon exclaimed, "He sit for inside!" He pointed straight ahead.

The stranger loosened his grip and eyeballed Salomon, enough to cause him recurrent nightmares. Salomon, still at his mercy, clasped his hands—rubbing them back and forth—pleading for mercy! Satisfied, he shoved Salomon aside and made his way to the office ahead. The meeting in the office was brief since it was an update from Ejiofor. Aloy escorted the stranger to the door, and the man's departure was swift.

Aloy stepped back inside, but on second thought, the cool breeze that swept past was soothing, so he turned back and sat outside the entrance of the building. *Not a bad idea,* he thought. Seeing pockets of activities and people in motion provided a temporary escape from despair. Before long, he spotted Ma Belle strutting down the left of the crossroad a few yards from his office building. He was disturbed upon sighting her and unsure of how much she saw a while ago. She was of average height, with a complexion on the darker side of brown, graced with a lengthy, full-bodied hair. With every stride, her generous hips swayed gracefully from side to side to the delight of onlookers. In looks, she was deceiving, but her news tasted like bile. Ma Belle had no favorites, but she had a predilection for those who "watered her palms" in search of relevant information. Notwithstanding a few embellishments, everyone wondered how she got firsthand information that was accurate.

Aloy's gaze met Belle's, and it was as if he had seen a ghost. She waltzed through patches of sticky, red earth, and puddles in his direction. And as she drew closer, his face glistened from the warmth of the sun while his eyes darted about. Pleasantries were brief and cordial as Aloy was eager to make out the purpose of this visit. Ma Belle knew business was bad all over Bamenda, but she attempted to ask the rather obvious question.

She stood with arms akimbo and asked, "How business? I hope say everything dey go fine, fine."

Reluctantly, Aloy responded, "*Na* all man this strike affect…"

That was just the right buzzword to queue in Belle. "*Mon dieu!*" she exclaimed.

Unaware of the motives of Aloy and that of the one-time nocturnal emissary, she had to possess more than a bag of tricks to pierce through Aloy's thoughts. After all the mind games, Belle made the first move. With ease, she narrated to Aloy the news-making rounds of his alleged involvement in Patrice's overt neo-racketeering operations, which maimed residents aplenty. The news angered him. But what infuriated him the most was Patrice's accusation of Aloy taking part in the extortion from the petty traders at ungodly hours. Once the feeling of rage took its full course, he realized Belle was still talking, but he could care less at that point; her poison-laden words were already taking effect.

Aloy took great pride in his positive self-image and personal achievements. To learn of his disparaged reputation in the public was by far a bitter pill to swallow. Certainly, he would have preferred the lancinating pain from a dagger to his chest than to snuff out his reputation. It was, for him, a *coup de grâce!* On top of that, she reminded Aloy of the monies lost on a daily basis for allowing his company's van to lay fallow in Patrice's compound.

"How him fit take your motor just like that? I think say you no get mouth to talk."

He sprang to his feet like a feline whose tail was stepped on, numb to rational thoughts. "Jules!" he called out. And in no time, Jules appeared in a flash while Belle slipped away quietly. "Make you give me Patrice number," Aloy requested.

Jules dashed in and out and provided his boss with Patrice's phone number, and address just in case. He put a call through to his adversary, Patrice.

"Who be this eh?" Patrice asked.

"Aloy," he replied. "I be the manager for Locomotive."

A slight pause ensued. "Ahh, *masa, na* you be this?" Patrice asked.

After all the phony pleasantries, Aloy went on to ask when he could pick up his vans and receive the cash balance from previous rentals. He asked Aloy to meet him at his residence to pick up the money at the end of business day by 6:00 p.m.

Jules beckoned Aloy not to go alone, but all fell on deaf ears. He motioned Jules to leave his presence and glanced at his watch, it was 5:03 p.m. Once more, he pondered, probed, and prodded his inner man in search of answers, but his scorned ego muzzled his introspection—it returned a blank retort. It was now 6:00 p.m. He called Jules and left him with a few instructions. Like Horatius of ancient Rome, Aloy was prepared to face the fearful odds in the temple of his gods. So he set out to meet his debtor.

*****

Day twelve

At the square, the sight was chaotic. While miscreants were hauled into the police van in handcuffs, plans were already hashed out for a massive ITU protest at 1800 hours. The instructions were to converge in Freedom Square before proceeding to the City Council. What once started as the Awala man's struggle gained quite a number of sympathizers. For some, the protest was a genuine cause while for others it was an opportunity to criticize the government for the perceived marginalization of the people of southern Cameroons—whose fate was sealed when they opted to join La République following the plebiscite of 1961.

Typically, the struggle for liberation depends, to a large extent, on the collective resolve of a people—provided all and sundry rise above personal egos for the actualization of the paramount goal—freedom. Faces, skin color, and gender do not mean a thing insofar as the objective remains on course. So it was only natural for security operatives to blend in with the emerging movement. Information, no matter how small, was important. Intelligence personnel planted within the mix relayed the details of the planned protest to listening ears over at the police headquarters. Two units of the anti-riot squad were mobilized and were on standby, waiting for the latest order. Additionally, special forces were on hand for reinforcement if the need arose. At half past six o'clock, what seemed to begin as a trickle of protesters evolved into a mammoth gathering of irate individuals. In no time, the gamut of emotions ran high and was eerily palpable.

*****

Patrice's residence, 6:30 p.m.

Aloy arrived at the location. He had no idea of what to expect, but sure enough, he was determined, at least, to get his money back. Just ahead of him, a footpath traversed the shin-high expanse of grassland into fairly equal halves. The path led to a few blocks of flat and an uncompleted two-story brick building surrounded by a high wall. The wrought iron, double-swing gate situated at the entrance was reinforced with iron rods running parallel on each side of the panel. On either side of the footpath, two majestic mahogany trees towered above shrubs and rooftops. The view of the setting sun and its rays bouncing off the fringes of the branches were breathtaking. Not even a thousand painters, past or present, could replicate such details with aplomb; the site was undoubtedly the canvass of an eternal painter!

Nevertheless, the feeling was fleeting. Two burly-looking men appeared in the distance, gesticulating to one another, which suggested a pleasant conversation. So far he was doing well with time. He continued along the footpath until both men were an arm's length away. Unexpectedly, they stopped and called out his name ecstatically with fervent fist pumps singing his praise, a manner befitting of a paramount ruler of their chiefdom. He was bemused but returned the compliments with firm handshakes and back-patting. Fair to say, one could have mistaken him for a pontiff from a distance. After all the adulation, he asked if they knew how he could find Patrice. Without hesitation, they pointed straight ahead in the direction of the brick building. He thanked them with a tip, and they departed.

He arrived at the house. Standing in front of the porch, he called out, "Patrice! *Na* me, Aloy. I *don* come."

Within a few seconds, a response emanated from the side of the building. To have a clear view of the person or where the response came from would involve him turning the corner to his right. Patrice appeared in a sky blue tracksuit, a headband to match, and a whistle around his neck. The movement he made with a light-walking pace suggested he may have been performing a calisthenics routine.

"Ah! See as you dress like say you be player for Canon Sportif Football Club, and you get whistle for neck," Aloy said, looking surprised. "Pa, you serious for this exercise, eh!"

"*Mon frère*, how we go do? With this *bele* all man for need stay in shape," replied Patrice.

Laughter erupted. Both shook hands and walked toward the entrance of the house. Patrice ushered him in and offered a glass of Bordeaux wine. What seemed to make for a good conversation was the current state of affairs. Any other discourse would have seemed forced or too mechanical. Patrice, after the second glass of wine, stretched the conversation a little.

"This Awala people think say them get we country. We must make sure them pack go their country."

Aloy responded, "I no fit blame them, government no fair at all."

"It be same thing you feel if government tax you big money and tax them small money," he said, taking a sip of his wine. "Make we all pay the same levy so business go continue..."

"No be so, Pa?" Aloy asked.

Patrice nodded deliberately and watched his visitor's countenance. "Ahhh! True talk, my brother," Patrice said. "I no trust these Awala people. They fit cause confusion for we place."

"Ah, ah, no talk so," Aloy interjected. "Them they contribute for we progress. See as different business plenty for we town."

"True talk, my brother," Patrice responded. "But that be the reason why they use their money buy small, small weapons to fight Popaul? On top that," he added, "them they move money for night..."

Aloy got wide-eyed in the middle of his last sip of wine; the sip took more than a few seconds to finish, biding him valuable composure time. *There was more to this coy statement from Patrice,* he thought, *a possible mole in-house or nearby divulged such information.* This was not the time to deliberate over these possibilities.

Aloy glanced at his watch and adjusted his posture as if to suggest he was ready to get to the matter of his visit. "Oh, *masa*, your money," Patrice said preemptively.

He soon reached for the closet close to the dining area, brought out a black bag, and dropped it in front of his guest. Aloy opened the bag and looked up. (Verifying an amount of money before leaving is permissible by culture.) Patrice nodded in approval, and Aloy counted seven hundred thousand CFAs; he closed the bag and rose to his feet. Both walked out of the house, and Patrice bade Aloy goodbye. Halfway through the narrow footpath—in between the two mahogany trees—he suddenly heard the sound of a whistle! It went off about three times. The events that unfolded thereafter were puzzling.

*****

City Council

From a distance, one could not help but notice Ejiofor's striking figure: he stood six feet tall, fair complexioned, with broad shoulders. Besides these features, what made him fearsome was his jet-black beard laced along his oblong-shaped face, gray eyebrows, furrowed glabella, and a gray streak of goatee running from the bottom of the lips to his chin could stare anyone into submission. Two parallel scars etched below his right cheekbone gave him a stone-cold look, a direct consequence of thirty-odd months of dogged fighting in the trenches of the then breakaway republic, Biafra.

As the crowd gathered, Ejiofor, the leader of the ITU, made his way to the stand at Liberty Square. He raised the megaphone in his right hand, brought it close to his mouth, and yelled, "*Ndi Igbo Kwenu!*" and with a loud cry, the crowd responded, "*Yaa!*"

Ejiofor spoke on behalf of the protesters. "We will no longer continue to tolerate the insensitivity of the so-called levy collectors… fairness and equity must prevail! Hear us loud and clear, today shall be the last of this ill-treatment and injustice."

The crowd erupted with a sustained applause. He raised his hand, turned sideways, as if to point in a direction, and said in a hoarse voice, "City council!"

And everyone turned in that direction and began chanting traditional songs used in war times. "*Nzogbu, nzobgu, enyinmba enyi…!*" If you asked anyone there what the outcome of the protest would be, no one was in doubt—a resolution. The crowd sang in deafening accord and hoisted placards of EQUAL RIGHTS AND JUSTICE; BAMENDA FOR WE ALL among others.

*****

Aloy had reached the end of the footpath when suddenly his ears propped up to hear the familiar war chant he was accustomed to in his days in Onitsha. He was elated because he knew the Igbo man never goes down without a fight. In his view, the end of the strike was in sight. He barely finished his thought when two men, whom he previously met on his way to Patrice, darted out of the thick shrubs. Before Aloy could raise an alarm, one stuffed his mouth with a handkerchief and secured it with duct tape while the other went for the bag of money. A violent tussle began, but none was able to keep him still.

In less than a few seconds, another man on a motorbike arrived. His part in the plan was to enable the attackers to escape. The man on the motorbike was fidgety. He screamed at his coconspirators to knock Aloy out cold because the protesters were inching closer from down the winding road, half a mile away.

The chant of "*Nzogbu, nzobgu…*" grew louder with every passing minute. It gave the already exhausted Aloy a second wind. The attackers wrestled, punched, kicked, and tugged, but they had met their waterloo. He fastened his grip on the bag while wrestling with one of the assailants on the ground. The crowd negotiated the bend on the adjoining street; now the distance to Jubilee Road was a few hundred yards. Short bursts of fleeting thoughts overwhelmed Aloy; that is, if he must die, the assailants must feel the protesters' wrath. One would think he was a wrestler in his heyday with what transpired next. By some means, he wriggled his hand off the grip and pulled the other assailant by the ankle; the assailant landed buttocks first. He was stunned for a second, then he rolled to the side, picked up a broken tree branch, and landed Aloy a blow on the left side of the head.

Unluckily for the assailants, some of the protesters were victims of the battering and extortion of Patrice's underground operations. "Catch them!" a few voices exclaimed! Swiftly, the crowd shifted attention to what was ahead of them. In a last-ditch effort, the exhausted assailants—cash in bag—peeled away from Aloy's grips. They made a short dash to the waiting motorbike and attempted to speed off.

The first responders to the seeming escape were the frontline protesters. Almost simultaneously, they bolted forward in hot pursuit of Aloy's attackers, like sprinters reacting to the sound of a gun. The rider swerved left and right in a bid to control the bike—they knew, of course, any fall would leave them at the mercy of the irate mob. Before the rider could gain control, the mob began pelting them with rocks of various sizes. The flights of rocks were parabolic, striking the heads and hunched backs of the bandits into a state of bewilderment. Finally, a jagged rock punctured the tires of the motorbike, and the impact plunged them into a near-fatal spiral. Still, with all the impact and near-death experiences, the bandits attempted to make a final dash on foot, but the gods of the land were determined to seal their fate. Two robust-looking ladies were approaching from the path down which the mobs and bandits were headed. Each put down a loaded basket of yams from their head, untied the wrappers around their waists, knotted them together, and ran the best twenty-five meters of their lives. With each holding one end, they stretched it to form a taut, horizontal line.

Everything happened so fast for the fugitives. By the time they realized what was ahead of them, they had run into the line. They spun the cloth around, and they tackled the men to the floor like rugby players. Out of breath, the fugitives succumbed. A cacophony of chants and applause filled the air!

But the moment was short-lived as the gendarmeries were on hand to prevent jungle justice; they confiscated the bag in their possession, handcuffed them, and hurled them into the police van.

Sirens blared, and the van reversed and raced to the station, leaving behind trailing dust.

*****

News filtered through to Mayor Etienne of the impending march to the city council. Before he could rally his staff to a safe location within the premises, the majority fled, and some were caught by barbed wires over the wall. Blood smears were noticeable on the walls while remnants of torn garbs swayed wherever the wind blew. A frantic mayday call was made to Lt. Col. Madakey who had command of the anti-riot squad. Within half an hour, the perimeter was secured; Madakey arrived at the scene with self-confidence.

As the chanting protesters inched closer and closer to their destination, the lieutenant colonel began speaking with the megaphone, "Please, exercise caution. Be reasonable. We are here to listen and address your grievances…"

The protesters responded, "Bamenda *na* for we all! No to levies! Equal rights and justice!"

Ejiofor motioned to the crowd to quieten down, but they kept chanting while he approached Lt. Col. Madakey in the company of the mayor. From the view of the crowd, and from a distance, one could see the gesturing hands, the moving lips, and disapproving nods of government officials; however, no one heard exactly what transpired during the conversation. In what looked like an impasse, Ejiofor waved his hand in disapproval and attempted to walk away but was called back. In less than ten minutes, an agreement seemed to have been reached. The three approached the crowd, and the cheers amped up in decibels. Again, Ejiofor motioned to the crowd, and the raucous cheers quietened.

"We hear your concerns. We feel your anger, but we must resolve the matter at hand as brothers and not enemies. Today, these one-sided levies cease to exist," the lieutenant said.

The crowd responded with deafening applause.

The lieutenant continued, "The mayor assures you that any future levies or taxes will be tendered to all businessmen or business owners in the marketplace."

Afterward, chants of "*Victoria acerta*" echoed across the valleys and highlands as the retreating protesters marched back to Freedom Square before dispersing.

*****

Last days

Days following the protest, Patrice and his cohorts were rounded up by Madakey in "Operation Restore Order." The strike was called off: business resumed at Bamenda City market, and restitution was paid to the ITU. Awala people's shops opened up, and sugar flowed through the land once again. Mankon town was taught a valuable lesson in hindsight. BL's expansive projects were suspended temporarily, but in the absence of Aloy, Kene held the fort. Besides, all vehicles belonging to BL—including those found in Patrice's premises—were impounded and transported to a holding facility to be claimed by their owner. The last time an eyewitness recalled seeing Aloy was when he was lifted atop a stretcher—in a frantic manner as though his life was hanging by the skin of his teeth—aboard an ambulance en route to the regional hospital.

Subsequently, the reprobates involved in the melee, as well as Patrice's henchmen, were handed over to Pierre who was to ensure due process of prosecution. Unfortunately for Patrice, karma never forgives. Constantine (Pierre's former boss), in the past, subjected Pierre to all manners of ridicule whenever he stood in the way of Patrice and his foot soldiers. To Pierre's chagrin, as often was the case, Patrice would splash a shot of whiskey in his face, which amused his boss. Pierre was to take his pound flesh this time. He paraded Patrice and his henchmen in handcuffs in an open-air lorry around the city's commercial district amid a jubilant crowd. The occupants of the lorry, upon command, help up signs which read ALL ROADS LEAD TO JAIL.

La resistance, according to intelligence reports gathered by the MOD, had gained wide acceptance in the southern region. The large-scale proliferation of sophisticated weaponry was on a scale like no other. The heavy-handed crackdown by security agents and the reprisal attacks by SPAM splinter groups led to senseless killings. With the government's nonnegotiable stance and the extrajudicial killings in the southern region, a full-scale civil war was moments away.

End

GLOSSARY

Pidgin English
bele—belly
don—it / is / has / have /am
kin'—kind
paye—country
pikin—little child/ the child of a man /someone's child
masa—master
na—is / it is
oga—boss/Mr./sir
wetin—what
wey—that

Some Igbo and Pidgin phrases (translations)

"Nzogbu, nzobgu, enyinmba enyi…!" (Trample to death, trample to death, forward-marching elephants.)

"Ndi Igbo Kwenu!" (Igbo people's clarion call to agreement, solidarity, or speaking in one accord.)

"Yaa!" (a response in agreement to the call).

"Which kin' problem be this? Why human beings no fit live in peace?" (What kind of problem is this? Why can't human beings live in peace?)

ABOUT THE AUTHOR

Ben O'Lee describes himself as a global citizen, whose early passion for storytelling was steeped in the fascinating stories of classical mythology, traditional musical and dramatic sketches, and listening to a rich blend of folklores. In his formative years, the allure for an unconventional worldview made living in America, the Caribbean, and Africa a treasured experience. In between writing, he is one who is passionate about the art of medicine and saving lives. As a history aficionado, he writes stories to etch everyday experiences in the minds of people by exploring alternative perspectives to enduring narratives. Through his writings, we are reminded of our shared experiences and compelled to think differently by engaging the power of our imaginations to revisit the past, embrace the present, and create the future.

CPSIA information can be obtained
at www.ICGtesting.com
Printed in the USA
LVHW051033040720
659731LV00004B/383

9 781647 016470